Your Comrade,
Avreml Broide

YOUR COMRADE, AVREML BROIDE

A Worker's Life Story

A NOVEL BY BEN GOLD

Translated by Annie Sommer Kaufman

Illustrations by William Gropper

A Yiddish Book Center Translation

WAYNE STATE UNIVERSITY PRESS
DETROIT

ISBN 9780814351383 (paperback)
ISBN 9780814352441 (hardcover)
ISBN 9780814351390 (e-book)

Library of Congress Control Number: 2024930767

On cover: Detail from the endpapers of the original Yiddish edition of *Avreml Broide* (1944). Illustration by William Gropper. Used by permission of the Gropper family. Cover design by Will Brown.

Publication of this book was made possible through the generosity of the Bertha M. and Hyman Herman Endowed Memorial Fund.

A Yiddish Book Center Translation

Wayne State University Press rests on Waawiyaataanong, also referred to as Detroit, the ancestral and contemporary homeland of the Three Fires Confederacy. These sovereign lands were granted by the Ojibwe, Odawa, Potawatomi, and Wyandot Nations, in 1807, through the Treaty of Detroit. Wayne State University Press affirms Indigenous sovereignty and honors all tribes with a connection to Detroit. With our Native neighbors, the press works to advance educational equity and promote a better future for the earth and all people.

Wayne State University Press
Leonard N. Simons Building
4809 Woodward Avenue
Detroit, Michigan 48201-1309

Visit us online at wsupress.wayne.edu.

Contents

Translator's Introduction   vii

Your Comrade, Avreml Broide   1

   First Part: The City of the Shtetl   5

   Second Part: The City of New York   53

Translator's Acknowledgments   119

Translator's Introduction

Once, when a fellow Gen-X acquaintance heard that I spoke Yiddish, he told me with pride that his grandparents had been successful actors in New York's Yiddish theater scene, but unfortunately, they had been in the wrong place at the wrong time, and through a misunderstanding, ended up blacklisted without cause during the Red Scare, becoming forced out of their profession. When I looked them up, I learned that they had been founding members of the ARTEF, the Yiddish theater troupe directly affiliated with the US Communist Party. Although this couple had boldly devoted their professional and creative energies to their ideals and political goals, their grandson inherited only an evasive and alienated image of them. This reluctance to accept the radicalism in a particular family reveals how successfully the second Red Scare cut off Americans from many of our most heroic ancestors, leaving us less empowered to fight for justice and liberation. I hope that by reintroducing *Your Comrade, Avreml Broide*, and its author Ben Gold, to English-language readers, we will access some of the lessons and legacies that have been hidden by political repression and cultural assimilation.

Your Comrade, Avreml Broide can be read as a formulaic Jewish American novel of immigration and acculturation, a 1944 installment between, for example, Abraham Cahan's 1917 *The Rise of David Levinsky*, and Philip Roth's 1959 *Goodbye, Columbus*. Gold's debut novel, however, gives us a principled hero who never falls for the false promise of the materialist American Dream and who avoids the disillusionment and alienation so prominent in those other stories of upward mobility. Instead, Gold's Avreml Broide explicitly rejects invitations from mentors, his wife's family, and the government, to enter the respectable middle class. Avreml does eventually "find his way" in America, but through striving for a better collective future and embracing loyalty to his union, his class, his people, and his party.

In 1944, when he became a published novelist, Ben Gold was at the peak of his status as a beloved and influential national labor leader, having achieved his own working-class version of the American Dream. In 1911, at the bar-mitsveh age of thirteen, Gold came to New York with his mother and sisters to join his father, who had arrived earlier to pay for their journey. In their native Bessarabia, at the southern edge of the Pale of Settlement (the western region of the Russian Empire to which Jews were restricted), the Gold family had been active in revolutionary movements. For a few months, Ben took odd jobs in factories making products like pocketbooks, cardboard boxes, and hats. When he started working as a sewing machine operator in a fur shop (until he grew tall enough to reach the cutting table), his father paid the union initiation fee so he could work at unionized shops. It was an important investment, as young Ben was the only family member employed at the time, and union wages made a difference. The following year, he was already serving as assistant chairman of his shop's union committee when the citywide union went on strike. Ben began taking on leadership roles as a picketer and patroller, sleeping near his shop to prevent scab workers from breaking the strike. That 1912 strike, as well as his sisters' activity in their own unions, brought Gold into the sophisticated visionary world of the Socialist Party. In 1916, at age eighteen, he joined the party himself, and in 1919, when the left wing of the party split off (and eventually became the US Communist Party), Ben went with them. He remained in the Communist Party through the first Red Scare, the Great Depression, and World War II, and became the main leader of the New York Fur Workers Union, and then, after mergers, the International Fur and Leather Workers Union. He survived numerous attacks and arrests and facilitated the union's transformation from a repressive American Federation of Labor (AFL) affiliated business collaborator into one of the boldest working-class forces in US history. Gold was especially proud of cutting gangsters out of the bullying role they had played under previous union administrations, maintaining political diversity in the union's leadership, bringing Greek and Black fur workers into the originally Jewish, Yiddish-speaking union, and joining with the leather industry and its even more ethnically and geographically diverse workforce.

We won't find explorations of Ben Gold's personality in his own writing, nor in politically aligned projects like Philip Foner's monograph history of the union. Instead, the two-page description in Irving Howe's pop-history blockbuster *World of Our Fathers*, nestled within a chapter excoriating the Communists for sabotaging the New York Jewish labor movement, provides the most evocative portrait:

> In the whole immigrant world there was no one quite like Ben Gold (1898–). Gold's natural setting was a meeting hall at Manhattan Center or a platform at Seventh Avenue and Twenty-eighth Street during lunch hour. With or without amplifier, he would rise to speak before thousands of garment workers milling about in the streets and ready for a few minutes of excitement: the followers whom he sent into transports of adoration, the opponents whom he scandalized, and those who savored his gifts with the neutral objectivity they might turn upon the technique of a great cantor.
>
> Physically, Gold was not an overwhelming figure at all. He was slight and, in his younger years, good-looking in a raffish sort of way. Quivering with nervousness, he experienced a kind of transfiguration when he opened his mouth, as if seized by some spirit of fury and negation. A stream of fire came pouring out of him, not always as grammatical speech, either in Yiddish or English (which he used interchangeably), and not always elegant, either; but as a rush, a flood of rage, summoning the anger of his listeners and teaching them they had funds of anger of which they had not even known.
>
> A virtuoso of invective, he poured endless scorn on the heads of the "Socialist fakers" and "AFL misleaders." Union rivals would remember with a tremor of astonishment his resources for *sheltn*, a Yiddish verb connoting curse, denounce, excoriate. When Gold reached "*dem tsentn shtok*," the tenth floor of the *Forward* building,

where Abraham Cahan had his office, there tumbled out of him arias of abuse as his voice, always high and thin, rose to a piercing shriek. His hysteria ate into his audiences, and they reveled in it, they found it bracing and cathartic, they gained some vicarious strength from it.

Part of his power derived from the ideological energies of Bolshevism, but part, too, had indigenous sources in the turbid streams of Jewish apocalypticism. Anyone familiar with east European Jewish history would not have found it difficult to imagine Gold as a disciple of the would-be messiah Jacob Frank, predicting an end to days and an escape from mundane torments, in a voice that leapt through the higher octaves of yearning and release.[1]

If Gold offered *Your Comrade, Avreml Broide* as an injection of working-class pride into the insecure milieu of Jewish American literature, he also wrote it to honor the books that shaped him. He claimed to have surprised himself by writing a novel, noting "I had never attended any lectures on literature. I had not even read many books, because I never had the time!"[2] But this denial, whether humble or self-aggrandizing, is contradicted by Foner's report that as a boy, Gold attended night classes at the Manhattan Preparatory School, hoping to study law, and that he "read Dostoevsky, Gorky, Zola, Tolstoy, De Maupassant, and drank deeply of the socialist writings of Jack London, Eugene V. Debs, Upton Sinclair and others."[3] Even if his union leadership duties had only afforded him the time to read the daily Communist Yiddish newspaper, the *Morning Freiheit*, he would have continued to encounter quality literature, because it consistently published the best of modernist Yiddish prose. Gold the reader trained Gold the writer and speechmaker, and he expressed himself in a range of styles: stirring tirade, absurdist sarcasm, casual familiarity,

1   Irving Howe, *World of Our Fathers: The Journey of the East European Jews to America and the Life They Found and Made* (New York: Simon and Schuster, 1976), 339.

2   Ben Gold, *Memoirs* (New York: William Howard Publishers, 1983), 197.

3   Philip Foner, *The Fur and Leather Workers Union: A Story of Dramatic Struggles and Achievements* (Newark: Nordan Press, 1950), 73–74.

and heartfelt sincerity. He wrote well in both Yiddish and English, but preferred Yiddish for longer pieces, such as fiction and his memoirs, which a comrade then translated.

Gold explicitly dedicated *Your Comrade, Avreml Broide* to the needle-workers who had died fighting against the fascists in the Spanish Civil War, where he set the novel's conclusion. Even so, much of the second part of the book imparts a nostalgic commemoration of the peak of the Furriers Union's power in 1926, when it triumphed in a bold strike and, among other ambitious gains, won the first forty-hour work week contract in the United States. The strike in New York made such assertive demands for reduced hours, increased wages, and improved working conditions, that the AFL-affiliated International Union intervened to undermine the New York fur workers. Gold's radical left ascendancy threatened to upset the balance of power that benefited the right-wing labor leaders and their Socialist Party allies, so they negotiated a weaker contract behind Gold's back to sabotage the success and popularity of the local Communist leadership. The rank and file did not accept that six-day week contract. Instead, they organized a citywide solidarity movement and threatened a general strike. The movement succeeded in establishing the forty-hour, five-day week for the fur industry, allowing Jewish workers to keep their Saturday sabbath and setting a precedent for the rest of the garment industry and all workers. In response to this left-wing victory, the right-wing, backed by the AFL leadership, removed Gold and his board from citywide union leadership and refused to enforce the new contract. When the workers struck in 1927 to reinstate the 1926 contract, the right appealed directly to the police department and hired gangsters to intimidate the picketers. Together, the police and gangsters brutally assaulted the striking furriers, who were arrested en masse, like in the penultimate chapter of *Avreml*. The 1926 strike remains a touchstone for the US labor movement, a high point of stridency and working-class solidarity during a period when most unions collaborated with employers and made few demands.

And I Obeyed

If Gold wanted to celebrate the triumph of his union's 1926 strike, process heartbreaking factionalism within the Communist Party, and honor comrades who fought and died in Spain, why write a novel rather than a history or a testimonial? Writing fiction gave Gold a medium in which to explore the personal emotions, desires, and relationships that motivated participation in revolutionary activities. In his other writing, speeches, personal letters, and even in his memoirs, he avoided personal topics. His memoirs passionately recount each dramatic twist and turn of every political negotiation, but—beyond her inclusion in their dual portrait on the frontispiece—do not even mention his wife (Sadie Algus, daughter of a Furriers Union leader.) He explains the experience of writing this novel while sick with the flu, not as a personal outlet for his creativity, but in terms of duty: "The people who were waiting there, inside the book which I had begun to write, were asking me not to leave them in the middle of their story, and I obeyed."[4]

Though he refused to "write about my personal problems"[5] in his own memoirs, in *Your Comrade, Avreml Broide*, Gold writes tenderly of interpersonal dynamics, especially of Avreml's and Miriem's courtship and crisis, where he explicitly acknowledges that the personal and political are interdependent. In chapter 2:8, when Avreml internally processes the conflict between his marriage and his faction-riddled party, he names his personal life as a liability to effective organizing. "He knew from his own experience that in the mass organizations, the workers have to think of Communists' personal lives as a reflection of Communist morale and accountability, and that the party's enemies are always looking to take advantage of the smallest blot in a Communist's personal life in order to smear the entire party." In reaction to this kind of emotional repression in Old Left thought, second-wave feminists of the next generation would

---

4   Gold, *Memoirs*, 198.

5   Gold, *Memoirs*, 5.

reframe the relationship between the personal and political as a source of strength, not a weakness.

Avreml's sense of conflict and loss as he cuts off his closest friends throughout his development into a fully realized Communist suggests an intriguing ambiguity that Gold may only have felt able to explore in the form of a novel. Although this bildungsroman has much in common with Soviet realist examples from the same time, with its emphasis on political growth and sacrifice on the path to "consciousness," Gold takes advantage of the genre's opportunities for interiority and uncertainty. In naming the book *Avreml Broide: A Worker's Life Story*, Gold honored the role of the individual while emphasizing his class loyalty and refusal to accept bourgeois social climbing as the American Dream. While in Europe, Avreml fantasized about opening his own workshop and going by the more formal name Avrohom in the New World. However, in America, and in the book's title, he keeps the humble diminutive version of his name even as he grows up. I don't expect Avreml's name to be as legible to English-language readers, so I amended the title to honor his identity as "Your Comrade." I hope that adding this status to the book's name opens provocative questions about how we relate to Avreml as our activist ancestor.

To Avreml, "his entire youth seemed an incidental, foreign phase of his life," but an attentive read of the first half of the novel, a portrait of his community of origin, can amplify the narrative's full arc. The circuitous first part, with its multiplicity of characters and timelines, can be read as a version of the rabbinic rhetorical technique of *p'sichta*, whereby an author winds through disparate texts to pick up relevant themes before arriving at the topic the audience anticipates. America and the union radicalized Avreml, but like Gold, he had learned many of his core values from his family and his Bessarabian village. Characters like Abish the Bear, Berke Blizzard, Nachmen Leib, and Bentshik model a range of options to young Avreml for how to grow into manhood. Their relationships with one another introduce the themes of exploitation, criminality, loyalty, and bravery, which guide Avreml as he grows into a reconfigured masculine ideal in New York. Gold's sensitive explorations of the class, gender, ethnic, and political dynamics of the old country show American readers that life and literature do not begin at Ellis Island, and that as much as a worker like Avreml may "become a new man" through their immigration and radicalization experience, their origins continue to shape our contemporary communities.

The European portions of the book, including the finale in Spain, tie the local and immediate struggles of the New York section of the Furriers Union into a powerful internationalist, Communist framework. The tsar's prison system was not irrelevant to the generation of workers who faced off with the employers, police, and right wing of the union in the 1926 strike. The fascist takeover of Spain half a decade earlier still burned for American readers in 1944. Gold could assume that his readers knew union comrades who had traveled from the United States to Spain between 1936 and 1938 to fight in the war with the Abraham Lincoln Brigade, which was semi-covertly organized by the Communist International and included many New York Jews. They knew all too well how accurately Avreml's final appeal from Spain anticipated the "enormous tragedy that is growing to threaten the entire world," as they mobilized to defeat Hitler's conquest of Europe. And certainly, the campaign to maintain the cohesion of the US Communist Party, as portrayed in the later section of *Avreml*, proved to be a pressing theme as the global Cold War enabled the United States to gut the Furriers Union and other militant forces in the labor movement.

In both of Avreml's worlds, Gold explores criminality and provides a nuanced spectrum of the concept. Both Avreml and his father Abish make a moral choice to disavow the underworld, but in Europe, criminals can embody values of loyalty and family, whereas in America they are only motivated by status and greed. There is an innocence to the Bessarabian thieves, who steal material objects and have barely any political consequence beyond provoking the non-Jewish peasantry or falling into the tsar's prisons. In America, Gold has absolutely no sympathy for gangsters, whom he depicts as vulgar buffoons at the service of corrupt union leaders, greedy bosses, and the brutal police force. When he rose to leadership in 1925, Gold set a top priority to rid the Furriers Union of the gangsters who extorted and oppressed the workers. The union meeting where Avreml witnesses gang rivalry may seem caricatured, but the Furriers

Union did have to contend with several real-life crime organizations, including the Murder, Inc. consortium and their colorfully named members. In his memoirs, Gold catalogs a list "of the underworld characters who were invited to help the [right-wing] union destroy the Communists, 'Big Alex,' 'Moishe the Babe,' 'Bullet-proof Harry,' 'Billy the Yak,' 'Sheenie Mike,' 'Chinaman Charlie.'"[6] Avreml, like Gold, is disgusted by such figures, but the novel doesn't even include the most notorious attacks by gangsters on the union. Both occurred in 1933, when Murder, Inc. assassinated union organizer Morris Langer by car bomb, and affiliated gangsters stormed the main union office trying to seize control on behalf of the AFL union. The fur workers beat them off, but two were killed. On the other side of the criminality equation, Gold shows the perversity of the government's authority to define legality. When the district attorney reads his "long list of illegal acts" in order to vilify Avreml, we readers understand the charges, which include striking and eviction defense, to be heroic, not criminal. His subsequent imprisonment ironically marks a milestone for him, helping him finally complete his transformation into "a loyal son of his class and his people."

Because Gold wrote this book for his own comrades, in their own language, and it was published by his community's newspaper, the *Morning Freiheit*, he didn't have to define his terms or give many details about each episode and historical figure. For twenty-first–century English-language readers, however, fleshing out some of the conflicts that the novel relates can help us appreciate the drama of Avreml's experiences and imagine how it felt for its original audience to read a story so similar to their own. It helps to know that the twentieth-century American Yiddish Left had two wings: the Communist left and the Socialist right. The left-wing solidified in 1919, when, in the wake of fierce debates on World War I and the ensuing Bolshevik Revolution, it split off from the Socialist Party to found the US Communist Party. Though both groups aspired to build a fully Socialist society, the right wing kept the name "Socialist" for their political party and cooperated with business owners, while the left wing received their new title "Communist" from the Soviet Union and

6   Gold, *Memoirs*, 91.

considered the Socialists capitalist collaborators and sellouts. The distinction carries a lot of weight and shapes Avreml's disillusionment in the end of chapter 2:3 and beginning of 2:4. The schisms continued in 1922, when the *Morning Freiheit* newspaper split off from the right-wing *Daily Forward*, and in 1930, when the left-wing International Workers Order split off from The Workers Circle,[7] a comprehensive mutual-aid network. In labor organizing, right-wing unions aligned with the craft-oriented AFL, while left-wingers, depending on directives from Moscow, either organized their own Communist unions, or, as in the Fur Workers Union, won leadership of the industry-wide union.

The engaging narrative of *Your Comrade, Avreml Broide* can escort readers through these major phases of US leftist history. At his initial union meeting, an electrifying speech by a Socialist Party politician called Mr. M, a reference to Meyer London, made Avreml feel for the first time in his life "that he was truly seeing the world in its full light" and launched his political transformation. Gold's depiction of London, who represented New York's lower east side in the US House, comes through as more respectful than may be expected, considering how London remained in the right wing of the Yiddish Left and betrayed the Fur Workers Union in the 1926 strike. Nevertheless, possibly because he died shortly thereafter, he remained an important figure for Gold and the Yiddish Left as a whole. In the introduction to his memoirs, Gold features a six-page portrait of London and one of their earliest meetings, when London advised "I tell you, Ben Gold, defend and protect workers! Always be on the side of the wronged." Like Avreml, Gold left his encounter with London "elated."[8] Then, at the height of the 1926 strike, when Gold, as manager of the New York Joint Board, was boldly negotiating for the forty-hour week, London hosted the contract negotiation behind the strikers' backs with the right-wing leadership of the International Union. Gold denounced London's role in this episode as a "vile betrayal."[9] Nevertheless, when he wrote *Your Comrade, Avreml Broide* in 1944, Gold included only the

7   Called by the English name Workmen's Circle until 2019.

8   Gold, *Memoirs*, 13.

9   Gold, *Memoirs*, 62.

flattering portrait, and in his 1983 memoirs asked himself why his one-time hero remained in the Socialist Party instead of joining the Communist: "Who knows? Didn't his conscience trouble him that he had betrayed his sacred ideals? Or did he lose his conscience?"[10]

After disillusionment with how the right wing of the union depends on gangsters and with Socialists' allegiance to business interests, Avreml joins the Communist Party and devotes himself to their complete program, including the Trade Union Educational League (TUEL). The TUEL, run by William Z. Foster, coordinated the Communist International's labor-organizing campaign to "bore from within" and press existing unions to become more radical and aligned with Communist goals. Gold's election as manager of the New York Joint Board of the Furriers Union in 1925 was in line with this strategy. In 1928, after seven years of this strategy, the Moscow-based Communist Party shifted to its Third International platform and rejected any sort of united front with capitalists and liberals. To accommodate, the network became the Trade Union Unity League (TUUL) and pursued "dual unionism," requiring Communist workers to organize separate Communist unions in each industry. This Third International period, as part of Stalin's consolidation of power, also rearranged the leadership of the US Communist Party, replacing Jay Lovestone (referred to as L in *Avreml*), a Lithuanian-born rabbi's son, with American-born William Z. Foster (Comrade F) as its secretary, provoking the Lovestone faction to break off, a drama which Avreml feels acutely. In 1934, the party reversed from dual unionism, disbanded the TUUL, and permitted American Communists to join and influence non-Communist unions, participate in the New Deal, and fight fascism in a popular front with other progressives.

Ben Gold went along with all these tactical shifts. He remained obedient to the decisions of the centralized Communist International, though he always preferred a unified, democratic union that included non-Communists over the tactic of running a separate, purely Communist union. The incessant factionalism, especially the activities of the Lovestoneites, took a toll on him, and he carried feelings of betrayal,

---

10 Gold, *Memoirs*, 17.

disappointment, and disgust throughout his life, some of them as very personal losses. The Lovestone faction cost Gold his best friend, Aaron Gross, with whom he served on the union's executive committee beginning in 1919.[11] In 1929, while Gold was focused on dual unionism work across the country, Gross led a furriers strike in New York to devastating failure. Ultimately, Gross joined the Lovestone faction and left the union, which must have broken Gold's heart. He died a year later, still injured from a police beating in 1927, which may inform the violence of the strike depicted in *Avreml*'s second to last chapter. The Lovestone faction dwindled until its dissolution in 1941, with Lovestone and many of his followers eventually becoming active anti-Communists. Avreml's anguish over his wife Miriem's participation in the Lovestone faction may be an echo of Gold's experience of losing Gross.

And on whom did Gold model Avreml Broide? According to the editor of the *Freiheit*, Paul Novick, the title character symbolizes the "unknown furrier," and brings a human scale to the generically heroic image of the fur workers by outlining a specific origin story and experience. This may have been Gold's literary intention, but coincidentally or not, his hero also shares many biographical traits with the union's popular longtime business agent,[12] Jack Schneider. Like Avreml (and Gold), Schneider grew up in Bessarabia, though he spent a few years in Palestine where he was pushed out of the union there for advocating cooperation between Jewish and Palestinian workers. He arrived in New York in 1921, around the same time as Avreml, and joined the left wing of the Furriers Union after encountering the right's tactic of gangster terrorism. He was popular with union members of all political affiliations, supported diversity of membership, and consistently received the highest election margins of any union officer (including Gold.) As a leader in the 1926 strike, Schneider became a frequent target of beatings by the police and the bosses' hired muscle. Finally, in 1939, the employers and the city government mounted a successful campaign to frame and imprison him for coercion. The shop that

---

11 Howe, 340. Foner, 325.

12 A citywide elected union officer who interacted with business owners to enforce their contract with the union.

issued the complaint against him was run by a fascist foreman who went to work wearing a Nazi SS uniform, as Avreml mentions in his courtroom testimony. The union mounted a mass movement to "Free Jack Schneider," but he was sentenced to prison, from where he was reelected as business agent. On his release, the fur workers paraded Schneider through the fur market in a scene similar to Avreml's homecoming. In style, *Your Comrade, Avreml Broide* may be an archetypal bildungsroman more than an accurate biography of a specific person, but Gold continued to praise his comrade, as in his memoirs, where he wrote "until the last moment of his richly honored life, Jack remained a highly principled and devoted citizen of the class-conscious, huge segment of the working class which fought for freedom and for justice."[13]

Important figures in Gold's own life, including London, Gross, and Schneider, informed the lessons he made sure Avreml learned through his relationships. The main characters Avreml turned to for emotional and political engagement, Morris and Miriem, proved to be inadequate and betrayed the movement. For his own part, Gold held fast to his commitment to the Communist Party, even through some of its most challenging times. He served on its US Central Committee from 1936–1948, although, like many Jews, he wavered in 1939 when the Soviet Union signed a non-aggression pact with Nazi Germany.[14] It is not clear how much Gold or other American party members knew about Stalin's systematic murders and imprisonments of Jewish artists and activists, but a public non-aggression pact with Hitler was enough reason to make any Jew rethink their loyalty to Stalin.

Gold's anxieties about loyalties and denunciations shape *Avreml*'s narrative. An exceptionally provocative scene, in which Avreml volunteers himself to be investigated by the party, had strong resonances to contemporary Communist and anti-Communist practices, as well as those in subsequent years of American political life. In the early 1930s, in an

---

13 Gold, *Memoirs*, 100.

14 Arnold Beichman, "The Communist Who Couldn't," *Washington Times*, March 25, 2007, accessed through https://web.archive.org/web/20071103203212/http://www3 .washingtontimes.com/commentary/abeichman.htm.

attempt to prove its antiracism, the US Communist Party held several public trials against party members accused of "white chauvinism," often framed around workplace conflict. The trials were well publicized spectacles, drawing crowds of up to two thousand people. Gold, who had dreamed of going to law school in his youth, served as chief prosecutor at least once. Such formalized, public opportunities to investigate and denounce disloyal members had already been used by the New York state government against the US left through the first Red Scare of the 1920s. Eventually, they metastasized into larger state-run campaigns such as the Soviet show trials in Stalin's purges, and the US government's House Un-American Activities Committee hearings during the Cold War. A similar energy can be traced through the New Left's "crit/self-crit sessions" in the 1970s, and to even more recent "accountability processes" and "call-out culture."

I Do Not Give Up My Belief in True Democracy

As mentioned above, the *Morning Freiheit* was the daily[15] Yiddish Communist newspaper, having broken off from the Socialist *Daily Forward* in 1922, in the journalism sector's iteration of the Yiddish Left schisms. The *Freiheit* went on to play important roles in politics, economics, and literature. It took its role as an exemplar of the Yiddish press seriously, always maintaining high standards of literacy. This devotion to Yiddish as a language set it apart from other papers, which used sloppier writing and assumed their readers were looking for something to read only until they succeeded in learning English. The *Freiheit* intentionally appealed to subscribers beyond the party faithful by becoming the leading newspaper for contemporary Yiddish literature and regularly featuring new works that occupied up to a third of the paper. Their weekend Literature and Art section profiled writers and featured poetry, and serialized novels also appeared frequently in any given issue. Although not serialized, their

---

15   Not technically a daily because it issued a weekend edition, not separate Saturday and Sunday papers.

publication of *Your Comrade, Avreml Broide* fit their literary agenda as well as their political one.

The *Freiheit* took its political role seriously as well, explicitly advocating for its allies in the left wing of the Yiddish Left, as it did for the Furriers Union. When international events threatened Jewish communities, notably the 1929 massacre in Hebron, and Stalin's non-aggression pact with Hitler in 1939, the paper initially wrote from a position of Jewish self-defense but ultimately acquiesced to pressure from Moscow and followed the party line in their reporting. Their unconvincing depictions of the Hebron massacre solely as Arab resistance to British colonialism, and of the non-aggression pact as a sincere gesture for peace, lost them substantial credibility and readership. Maintaining party loyalty as a Yiddish newspaper was a tricky commitment, especially as the Soviet Union persecuted Jews and Israel grew to play a central role in American Jewish culture and politics.

Under party influence during World War II, the newspaper expanded to create a membership organization, The Morning Freiheit Association, which managed and promoted its political and cultural work. Ben Gold sat as the president, bestowing his popularity and union credibility, but party operative Alexander Bittelman ran the project as its executive secretary. Ukrainian-born Bittelman had been a founding member of the US Communist Party in 1919, and Foster's primary strategist through the factionalism of the 1930s. Recognizing the important role of Jewish Americans during the war, party leadership assigned Bittelman the task of building Jewish support for Communism through the paper and its extensions. The historian Melech Epstein, who had been a *Freiheit* writer and editor before leaving the party over the Hitler–Stalin pact, called the Morning Freiheit Association "the center of Jewish communism," which "comissarlike, [Bittelman] dictated."[16]

Publishing *Your Comrade, Avreml Broide* was one of the Association's first significant endeavors during its inaugural year. It regularly published

<hr>

16 Melech Epstein, *The Jew and Communism: The Story of Early Communist Victories and Ultimate Defeats in the Jewish Community, U.S.A. 1919–1941* (New York: Trade Union Sponsoring Committee, 1959), 401. Accessed through marxists.org.

political pamphlets, often speeches of Bittelman's in separate Yiddish and English versions, but a hardcover, illustrated, original novel, which had not been offered serially, was a notable and ambitious project. However, they had an already established team, and publicity was a cinch through the newspaper. The rookie author was the beloved president of the Morning Freiheit Association, and both the editor, Naphtoli Buchwald, and the illustrator, William Gropper, were Freiheit staff members.

In William Gropper, the project had one of the most prolific and successful visual artists to come out of the American Yiddish Left. He was born to Yiddish-speaking immigrants in New York City's lower east side, where he watched his mother sew piecework at home and mourned his aunt's death after the Triangle Shirtwaist Factory fire. He himself dropped out of public school at fourteen to work in the garment industry as a "bushel boy" distributing materials to sewing machine operators. Over the next few years, he studied art at the anarchist Ferrer School under Robert Henri and George Bellows, until Frank Parsons, the director of the New York School of Fine and Applied Art, arranged a scholarship for him to study there and learn more traditional, commercial techniques. After graduation, Gropper embarked on a successful and influential career in journalism as an illustrator and cartoonist. He worked for some mainstream publications, including *Vanity Fair* and W.R. Hearst's *New York American*, where he regularly illustrated Robert Benchley's column. Much of his work however, supported the radical left. He helped found the *Rebel Worker* newspaper with the Industrial Workers of the World, and the *New Masses* magazine, which was affiliated with the Communist Party. As the primary staff artist for the *Morning Freiheit*, he illustrated news stories and provided editorial cartoons, often audaciously caricaturing the right wing of the Jewish Left, especially their favorite target Ab Cahan, the editor of the *Forward*.

In 1927, Gropper and his wife Sophie were invited to the Soviet Union to celebrate the tenth anniversary of the Bolshevik Revolution. They stayed a full year and traveled through the Russian countryside, where he sketched villages and landscapes, presumably informing his illustrations of Avreml's Bessarabian shtetl. Gropper developed a consistent oil painting practice in the 1930s and began showing annually at the influential modernist ACA

Gallery beginning in 1936. He illustrated numerous works, including a union pamphlet with Gold in 1931, a poetic testimonial to the Warsaw Ghetto Uprising with Howard Fast in 1946, and several books of his own, notably a foundational graphic novel called *Alay-Oop* in 1930, which was republished in 2019.[17] His stature continued to grow, with 1937 bringing a Guggenheim Fellowship, murals for the Works Progress Administration, and purchases by the Metropolitan Museum and the Museum of Modern Art. His success as a painter, along with constraints on press illustration, such as the rise of photography and the pressures of the Red Scare, led to his resignation from the *Freiheit* in 1948 and his departure from the journalism field entirely. The full-page illustrations and doodly "adornments" he created for *Your Comrade, Avreml Broide* show him in this transitional phase between sketched political caricature and large-scale emotional paintings. They provide bold energy and evocative images ranging from tender family moments to expressionistic battle scenes.

Gropper was one of two visual artists called to testify before the House Un-American Affairs Committee in 1953. He appeared, but limited his testimony to pleading the Fifth Amendment, and was subsequently blacklisted from galleries and government agencies, thwarting his career as he was at the peak of his craft. To process his experience through what he called the "American Inquisition" Gropper worked for three years on a stunning series of fifty lithographs based on Goya's *Los Caprichos*, a full set of which are housed in Wayne State University's art collection. Gropper's *Capriccios* are luridly hellish, decrying many forms of destruction, including the exploitation of the garment industry, the brutality of war, and the ruthlessness of the rich and powerful in business and government. As the Red Scare waned in intensity, Gropper recovered some of his success as a painter, being reaccepted to the New York gallery scene by 1961. He turned to explicitly Jewish themes in response to the Holocaust, even designing biblically themed stained glass windows for a suburban Chicago synagogue. He maintained his politically artistic activity up until his death in 1977, leaving a colorfully chaotic series depicting the Watergate hearings, and a powerful legacy of work.

---

17   William Gropper, *Alay-Oop* (New York: New York Review Comics, 2019).

Your Comrade, Avreml Broide went through two printings at Prompt Press, the Communist Party's official print house in New York, and sold eight thousand copies.[18] The *Morning Freiheit* promoted its product in the paper through articles and advertisements and at events. At the newspaper's anniversary celebration at Carnegie Hall, the Morning Freiheit Association presented Gold with the book's first copy, a photograph of which was featured with an extensive review in the weekend Literature and Art section. The paper's editor in chief, Paul Novick, wrote the review and shared his frank opinions of its intentions, strengths, and weaknesses.[19] Novick loved the first part of the novel, set in Bessarabia. He identified Gold's "leit-motif" in the conclusion to the first chapter, as the townspeople participate in Berke Blizzard's protests against the greedy landlord: "You give it to him, Berke! Keep at it. Scream for all of us." Novick found the parallel between Gold and Berke Blizzard obvious, wondering how much Gold could even identify with Avreml, the everyman worker. Novick appreciated Gold's depiction of union activity as the process through which Avreml, like masses of Jewish immigrants, became American, or as Avreml calls it, "found their way." In Novick's description, "they couldn't get used to this country. They wandered around as if in a world of chaos . . . The union made them true Americans, gave them a sense of the flavor of America, set them up as the builders of America, gave them a chance to participate in American traditions." Although the New York half of the novel, with all its episodic cataloging of union maneuvers and factionalism, may leave today's readers a bit dizzy, Novick wanted even more historical events included in this section. He thought that this second section may have seemed weaker because the episodes it described were "still alive before our eyes." He complained that ninety pages were not enough to cover every significant event from 1920 to 1938. He noted that the last chapters seemed rushed and figured that Gold ran out of time to write due to his union responsibilities. As it was, the *Freiheit* articles and Gold's memoirs defended his reputation for industriousness and dedication to the union by explaining that he only

---

18 Walter Bernstein, "Furriers' Gold," *New Masses* May 6, 1947, 14. Accessed through marxists.org.

19 P. Novick, "Ben Gold's Book 'Avreml Broide'," *Morning Freiheit* May 14, 1944: 6.

found the time to write when he was laid out sick from the flu, not by
shirking his union duties!

Even though the novel didn't have enough history to satisfy Novick
the newspaper editor, it assumes a breadth of specific knowledge on behalf
of the reader, and its language of publication likewise reflects its intended
audience. Publishing in Yiddish in 1944 shows not only that this was a
book intended for Jews but also for the older, Yiddish-speaking Jews who
had lived through the strike of 1926. Younger Jews hadn't been allowed
to immigrate to America after the drastic quotas legislated in 1924, and
the Jews born in the United States since then were less likely to have
been reading literature in Yiddish. By 1944, secular anti-assimilationist
activists, including the New York Fur Workers Union's cultural program,
had begun implementing Yiddish instructional programs for children and
adults, but the tide was turning. The *Freiheit* included occasional articles
in English and was already issuing a regular English supplement that
eventually grew into the monthly magazine *Jewish Life*, which publishes
now as *Jewish Currents*.

Beyond *Jewish Currents*, few organizations from this passionate and
powerful Jewish Communist world survived intact. The Holocaust, rev-
elations of Stalin's purges, Zionism, and the second Red Scare all weakened Jewish American endurance and faith in the Communist future.
The ruthless assault on Communists in the labor movement during the
1940s and '50s by the government, business owners, and business unions
crushed the Furriers Union and exiled Ben Gold, though he put up a good
fight. The Taft–Hartley Act of 1947 added many restrictions on union
tactics, and in an echo of the anti-Lovestoneite statement Avreml had
resisted signing, required union officers to sign affidavits declaring they
were not members of the Communist Party. After thirty years of loyal,
if challenging, membership, Gold was finally forced to leave the party.
When he wrote an open letter to acknowledge his compliance with the
Taft–Hartley provision in 1950, he didn't hide or equivocate. He took it
as an opportunity to resist and maintain his dignity:

> [Our] Union is one of the last unions to comply with the
> Taft–Hartley Law. Our union resents, rejects and condemns this

legislation as a slave labor Act which is contrary to every basic principle of democracy. [We] would never have complied with this slave labor law if not for the treacherous policies of raiding, wrecking and strike-breaking practiced by the top officials of CIO[20] and AFL who are utilizing this anti-labor law in order to destroy trade unions . . .

I belonged to the Communist Party because I have known it to be the working class party in America. The monopolists, bankers and profiteers have their own political parties which control the government. . . .

As a member of the Communist Party for 30 years, I found the thinking of the members of the Communist Party, its program and activities determined by one, and only one, burning desire— to serve the best interests of labor and the people, to end the cruel exploitation of the working people, racial hatred and bigotry, and to build up an economically secure, politically free, united, democratic and peaceful America. . . .

I have resigned from the Communist Party, but I do not give up my belief in true democracy.[21]

Despite this clear statement, the government did not accept Gold's resignation and indicted him for perjury. His trial dragged on for years, going through several appeals and bringing in ex-communist witnesses for the prosecution, including Benjamin Gitlow (The Drummer) who hadn't seen Gold for years. Former Congressman Vito Marcantonio served as his defense attorney until he died from a heart attack in 1955. The Supreme Court of the United States reviewed Gold's case in 1957 and repealed his conviction on a technicality. In 1965, after the labor movement had been sufficiently defeated and incapacitated, the court ruled the affidavit

---

20 The left-leaning Congress of Industrial Organizations expelled the Fur and Leather Workers Union in 1949, even though it was one of its founding members, and one of only two unions to win wage increases in 1948.

21 As quoted in Ann Fagan Ginger and David Christiano eds. *The Cold War Against Labor, Volume 1* (Berkeley: Meiklejohn Civil Liberties Institute, 1987), 427–428.

requirement of Taft–Hartley unconstitutional. The energy and attention that the trial demanded, along with the loss of allies such as the Congress of Industrial Organizations (CIO), and the relentless attacks of McCarthyism, drastically diminished the functionality of the Furriers Union, making Gold's leadership impossible. Although he was reelected to the union presidency in 1954, he resigned shortly thereafter and retired to Florida, after which the Fur and Leather Workers Union entered into a string of mergers, eventually yielding today's United Food and Commercial Workers (UFCW), one of the largest and most complacent unions in the AFL-CIO.

A year following the publication of *Your Comrade, Avreml Broide*, Gold had a collection of short stories ready. *Menchen* (People) offers mostly portraits of workers who come to the office of Ben Gold the union president to tell him their stories, and includes a variety of experiences with the union, war, class, and assimilation. Gold submitted the collection to the *Freiheit*, and although Bittelman responded that "you have here something that is even of greater value than your first book," the Morning Freiheit Association did not publish it. Perhaps Gold did not satisfactorily address Bittelman's warning about "several ideological angles that will have to be clarified."[22] Instead, the Needle Trades Workers Committee released the collection in 1949, again with illustrations by Gropper. Gold continued to write fiction through his forced retirement, novels published by volunteer book committees, and occasionally shorter pieces in literary journals. In a review of his 1970 book *In Those Days*, Ber Grin (pseudonym of A. Prints,) a writer who had served on the *Freiheit*'s editorial board, noted that Gold had accomplished "significant progress in style and substance" since the publication of *Avreml*. He even praised the new book as "an answer to those who complain and mourn that the novel has died."[23]

---

22 Letter from Alexander Bittelman to Ben Gold, February 27, 1945, International Fur and Leather Workers Union Records, 1913–1966. Collection 5676, Box 10, Folder 17.

23 Ber Grin, *From Generation to Generation: Literary Essays* (New York: Ikuf and Ber Grin Book Committee 1971), 363. Accessed through https://archive.org/details/nybc206855/.

Your Comrade

As a child, I spent my summers at Camp Kinderland, one of the last surviving institutions of *Avreml Broide*'s world. When I arrived in 1987, we sang old union songs, learned to write simple Yiddish words, and competed in the camp-wide Peace Olympics, each team representing a recent anticolonial movement. I was on Mozambique and helped my team perform the rap we wrote: "Portugal destroys, the girls and the boys . . ." I became fiercely devoted to Kinderland and to the movements of hope and struggle for which it prepared us. We understood ourselves as the children of the movement, inheritors of a heroic lineage, certain of how to answer the refrain of one of our favorite union songs, "Which Side Are You On?" Our buildings were named for ancestors of many eras, some from the milieu of Kinderland's founders, like the Yiddish sweatshop poet Morris Rosenfeld, and also for those from longer ago, like Harriet Tubman, and from farther away, like Pablo Neruda. One building displayed a large handkerchief scrawled with a message from Civil War Spain, where Kinderlanders fought fascism. When I read Avreml's letter from Spain, I immediately remembered that handkerchief and felt a strong sense of lineage.

Even so, the political era to which we referred most in the 1980s and '90s was to the '60s, to our parents' radical youth. Their songs, images, and slogans shaped our worldviews, whether we aspired to them or mocked them. My father, a Students for a Democratic Society (SDS) veteran who had aligned with the labor faction in the SDS split, sent me to Kinderland as a Jewish counterbalance to the political influence of my mothers' parents, religious-Zionist Holocaust survivors. Even though I encountered Yiddish on both sides of that divide, I still had to make a more intentional effort to learn the language when I came into adulthood. At Kinderland, some of the references to the '60s were explicit and righteous and I could make sense of the messages. At age eleven, I was on the team called "Mississippi Freedom Summer Nineteen Sixty-Four." We watched the *Eyes on the Prize* PBS series and practiced passive-resistance techniques, expecting to use them outside of camp in similar protests.

Other legacies from the '60s were too close to home and too fraught for me to recognize or understand. I knew several of my friends were somehow related, and it was whispered that their families were unavailable, or in prison, but I never heard about the Weather Underground, or sensed how the radicalism and sacrifices of the previous generation wounded and isolated some of the children with whom I sang and played kickball.[24] Even the specifically Communist origin story of Camp Kinderland wasn't discussed explicitly. Our directors decided to build a new bunk named after the *Morning Freiheit* but were still too shaken by the Red Scare to emphasize its Communist Party affiliation.

Translating *Avreml* has been an opportunity to sort out the contentious histories I encountered at Kinderland, where, like in the novel, I sensed some doubt and regret behind the overconfident messaging. Catching glimpses of my summer camp as I researched has helped anchor me through the party history that I find rather confusing and frustrating. It was sweet to find a letter in the Furriers Union archive inviting "Brother Gold" to Camp Lakeland (the section for grown-ups, next to Kinderland for children,) for Yom Kippur week of 1945. It was also affirming to learn that Gold mobilized three thousand veteran fur workers to go to Paul Robeson's concert at Lakeland/Kinderland and support him through what became known as the Peekskill riots of 1949,[25] an event I learned about as a child at our Paul Robeson Playhouse.

The language of *Your Comrade, Avreml Broide* has also called upon my specific strengths in Yiddish and English. I spent my first year out of college in Bessarabia, which is now Moldova, where I had the great honor of learning with Yekhiel Shraybman as his last Yiddish student. Bessarabian Yiddish has its own personality, with a distinctive squishy sound that Shraybman flaunted. When he read his own pieces with me, he taught me how carefully a writer crafts prose and enjoys the creative process. I now wonder if Gold and Shraybman read each other's work.

---

24 My fellow camper Zayd Dohrn recently produced an excellent podcast on his family's experiences: https://crooked.com/podcast-series/mother-country-radicals/.

25 Harold Cammer, "Taft-Hartley and the International Fur and Leather Workers Union," in Ginger and Christiano eds. 410.

Another influence I relied on while reading Gold were the reel-to-reel copies of the complete Warner Bros. film catalog available to me in college. I succeeded in watching every one of their movies released in 1933 and '34 to learn about how censorship changed the studio's content and style. It meant I watched a lot of gangster and "social message" pictures set in urban immigrant America. Those Warner Bros. movies, with their foreign accents, exaggerated gangsters, crooked businessmen, and lone working-class heroes acclimated me to the kind of English Avreml encountered. I could hear Gold's Bessarabian-American Yiddish in cinematic-American English with expressions like "phony," "racket," and "nothing doing."

As a novel portraying immigration and bilingualism, *Your Comrade, Avreml Broide* offered some fun challenges for translation into Avreml's new language. Gold plays with Avreml's exposure to and process of learning English, and I didn't want to lose that sense of confusion or the acknowledgment of his eventual proficiency. When Gold introduces a new English word, he transliterates it into Yiddish letters, and then sometimes translates it into a Yiddish term in parentheses: פּאָרצענטסעם (האָלבע לבנות). To show that these new English words are a part of Avreml's education, I spelled them out as I imagine he would pronounce them, with italicization and dashes between syllables, to mark for the reader how *for-in* (alien) they feel to him. When he listens to English dialogue that confuses him, as in the meeting with the gangsters who use a lot of heavily accented English, I followed Gold's lead and exaggerated dialect and unusual spellings. Gold uses some consistent vocabulary choices between the first and second parts of the book, so I tried to preserve those references and continuity while showing Avreml's gradual command of the English language.

Even when the book was released in 1944, as the *Freiheit* traced each battle of World War II daily, Gold wrote Avreml's letter from Spain to his comrades in order to send his readers a message. By setting Avreml's finale and martyrdom in the Popular Front period, before the Hitler–Stalin pact, Gold may be recovering his ideal iteration of Communist organizing. The fully realized comradeship which Avreml claims at the conclusion of the bildungsroman is entirely focused on the fight against fascism, and it is finally and triumphantly unencumbered by the temptations of compromise and personal relationships. Though we still have internationalist duties to fight fascism eighty years later, our organizing cultures have veered away from Avreml's macho acceptance of punishment and suppression of personal connections. Under the influence of feminists who joyfully equated the personal with the political, and the formulations of thinkers such as Mariame Kaba, who asserts that "my political commitments are to developing stronger relationships with people and to transforming harm,"[26] relationships have become the pinnacle, and at times, the sole stated purpose, of leftist organizing. I recently spent a season in the South Hebron Hills, in solidarity with Palestinians experiencing ethnic cleansing. At our group's initial orientation meeting, instead of vowing to "carry out our orders," as Avreml wrote from Spain, we set our primary intentions to "build relationships" with Palestinian communities and activists, and acknowledged that we will only succeed in our goals if we have "strong relationships" with each other.

As I read *Your Comrade, Avreml Broide*, with its overt veneration of party loyalty and subtextual sense of loss and doubt, I wonder how Gold squared his love of democracy and the Jewish people with Communist authoritarianism and Stalinism. In 1944, how much did he and other American Communists know about Stalin's murders of Jewish writers, artists, and so many others? Did Gold think that a strong Soviet state would protect workers in his own neighborhood, whatever the cost to Jews abroad? To consider his possible remorse is also to wonder why some Jews now still think that a strong state, even a "Jewish state" will protect us.

I hope that this fresh encounter with *Your Comrade, Avreml Broide* will help us reflect on current developments in both the labor movement and Jewish culture. Gold's story, with its convictions and its ambiguities, reminds us how high the stakes are and points to ways we can move forward. As we maintain our loyalties to Gold's democratic and visionary ideals, we do not need to sacrifice our personal and collective relationships.

---

26 Eve Ewing, "Mariame Kaba: Everything Worthwhile Is Done With Other People," *Adi Magazine*, Fall 2019.

Today's most successful organizers are bringing queer, feminist, and racial justice lenses to their comprehensive platforms and committing to the disability justice principle not to leave anyone behind. Workers are joining together to launch new unions and to push large established unions toward more democratic governance and confrontational demands. Within the UFCW, the members of Essential Workers for Democracy are pressing for the kinds of large-scale organizing campaigns and direct officer elections that built Gold's powerful Fur and Leather Workers Union, one of their direct forebears. American Jews are also rededicating a focus on democracy, both by fighting fascism in anti-racist coalitions, and by refusing to let self-appointed leaders speak for them. New Jewish organizations invest in learning, diversity, and the arts to find the belonging and safety that previous generations expected to find in nation states. Reading *Avreml Broide*, today's comrades can still "find our way" through organizing for a better world, a world of both loyalty and love.

Further Reading

Epstein, Melech, *The Jew and Communism: The Story of Early Communist Victories and Ultimate Defeats in the Jewish Community, U.S.A. 1919–1941*. New York: Trade Union Sponsoring Committee, 1959. Accessed through marxists.org.

Foner, Philip, *The Fur and Leather Workers Union: A Story of Dramatic Struggles and Achievements*, Newark, Nordan Press, 1950.

Gold, Ben, *Memoirs*. New York: William Howard Publishers, 1983.

Howe, Irving, *World of Our Fathers: The Journey of the East European Jews to America and the Life They Found and Made*. New York: Simon and Schuster, 1976.

Isserman, Maurice, *Which Side Were You On: The American Communist Party During the Second World War*. Middletown, Connecticut: Wesleyan University Press, 1982.

Le Blanc, Paul and Tim Davenport eds. *The 'American Exceptionalism' of Jay Lovestone and His Comrades, 1929–1940: Dissident Marxism in the United States, Volume 1*. Chicago: Haymarket Books, 2018.

Lozowick, Louis and Gropper, William. *William Gropper*. London: Art Alliance Press, 1983.

Ottanelli, Fraser M. *The Communist Party of the United States: From the Depression to World War II*. New Brunswick: Rutgers University Press, 1991.

Zumoff, Jacob A. *The Communist International and U.S. Communism 1919–1929*. Chicago: Haymarket Books, 2015.

Your Comrade, Avreml Broide

Dedicated to the American
needleworkers
who fell in Spain.

FIRST PART

THE CITY OF THE SHTETL

1

From afar, it was a shtetl, but to its residents it was The City. It was a Bessarabian city, with worlds unto itself, a city of healthy, young, iron-muscled blacksmiths who got fired up in fist fights between Jews and drunk peasants. Like a riot, they blasted out of their forges on Blacksmith Street and chased away the drunks on Market Street.

It was a city of tailors and shoemakers who could update the fine-looking propertied set, patch up the poor folk, and assemble ready-made clothes for the fairs. It was a city of clerks carrying entire shops in their heads. They knew how much their merchandise cost and for how much it could sell after a lengthy haggling. Those clerks had sharp minds, practiced eyes, and pencil-nibbling tongues. It was a city of great merchants and small shops, of learned Jews and coarse youths, of religious wives, and brazen broads, fat cats and paupers, philanthropists and cheapskates. A city like other cities.

But throughout the region, this city had a bigger name than others, thanks to its thieves. People told all sorts of stories about its thieves, many of them true, and even more of them made-up.

Spread along a valley, soaked in mud for much of the year, The City, or if you like—the shtetl—was surrounded by mountains, forests, and fields, trimmed with rivers, and immersed in orchards. Peasants traveled from every area in the region to sell their produce and buy merchandise there.

In that city, the residents had long become accustomed to Berke Blizzard's voice, and how on summer afternoons, it would rip with a shrill howl through the houses' open doors and windows, like a dull saw on a steel grate. Everyone knew that's just how Berke Blizzard talked, even in his most calm and restful tones. It got bad when Berke Blizzard became enraged, which happened fairly often. Then, his voice got even shriller and howlier, and each word carried across the length and width of the street like a cannonball. It became impossible to speak, and the street was compelled to fall silent. The hot words that gushed from Blizzard's shrill-howling throat, like from an iron kettle, filled the street with a racket, as if a thousand locomotives blared together, one joining the other. People would stop up their ears with both hands and utter a shocked "Lord, save us" as if protecting themselves from hot steam.

Rekhl was a good, quiet, small woman with deep wrinkles in her pale, gaunt face. On account of her husband's name, she was called Rekhl Berke Blizzard's. With quiet and measured words, which creeped slowly and modestly from her thin dry lips, she pleaded with her enraged husband: "Nu, that should be enough already. Haven't you boiled enough? I'm begging you. Don't you have a limit? For God's sake, have pity on your health. People are gathering like they would for a natural disaster. Please, stop your seething. I beg you. Have mercy."

Berke Blizzard would be quiet while his wife Rekhl made her plea, speaking as if she were reciting a prayer. For one thing, he had reverence for his Rekhl, the mother of his three dear children. He remembered her in her youth, when she was well known in town for her beauty and refinement, even though she had been raised in poverty and want. Second, he liked it when she begged him with her kind, quiet talk. And third, while his wife Rekhl was delivering her speech, Berke could catch his breath. But, as soon as Rekhl finished, he started over again in force, letting out a hail of hot bullets through the street, their screeches and howls silencing the street's normal bustle.

Berke would stand planted next to his wife's bagel and candy booth, with his hands shoved deep in his pants under his belt. The stance made his short, wide-shouldered body look even wider. His small, red, piercing eyes became even redder and more piercing, and screams and abuses hailed nonstop from his wide-open mouth.

Even when Berke had finished shouting all his grievances out, and finally submitted to the pleas and pacifications of his Rekhl's sweet words, and began to help her pack up the leftover bundles of bagels into sacks, the bagels strung on a cord like beads, and the candies wrapped in red, green, yellow, and blue paper with careful peaks on one side, and thin clipped fringes like little hairdos on the other side—even then, when Berke had stormed and blizzarded himself out, he would still occasionally fire out a last holler or squawk that had evidently remained stuck in his throat, burning like a hot coal.

Mostly, Berke's screams were directed against Nachmen Leib the moneylender, who extorted Berke's brother Faivish, and his four orphans. Faivish had lived on Tailor Street for twenty-two years, in one of the old houses belonging to Nachmen. Every Friday, Faivish the Tailor brought Nachmen his weekly payment. Nachmen accounted a portion of it as lodging fees, a portion as housing payment, and the rest, as payment of interest on his loan.

In addition to the weekly payment, Faivish served the moneylender and his entire household as their personal tailor. That work was separate from the settlement and not calculated in the financial accounting.

Berke warned his brother more than once about those kinds of payments. "This is going to end with Nachmen Leib taking your money and then throwing you out of the house. Mark my words Faivish, you won't get any warning spelled out in black and white from Nachmen Leib. He will simply pillage you."

And then he would continue arguing with his brother Faivish: "What good does this whole arrangement do you? Do you even call that a house? What it really is is a hovel. You patch one hole in the roof and three other holes open up. You've always got water pouring in, even when it's only drizzling outside. You're constantly mending the roof, and when a rain comes, you have to set out bowls and pots and trenches under the new holes. Oy, and the windows? They don't even have panes! And what's more, the cellar is all soaked and moldy. Mark my words Faivish, no good is going to come of this. Either the house will collapse, or Nachmen Leib will just loot you and throw you out on the street."

Faivish the Tailor, an emaciated and stooped man in his fifties with a sparse little beard, was the opposite of his younger brother Berke. He kept his tongue tied. He worked his whole life, obeying what people told him, and following what they ordered. Speaking was a torment for him. Making it worse, he mumbled, and that gave him grief. He always felt people were laughing at him. Only with his own brother, and especially on the topic of his house, was he not short on words.

"What are you talking about? What?" he pleaded with Berke. "What the hell do you mean Mr. Nachmen Leib is going to take the house away from me? Will he really? It's my house for crying out loud."

"It's your house, but you're still paying and patching, patching and paying," interrupted Berke.

"Of course I pay! Why shouldn't I pay? Every Friday I pay just as much as we agreed on. Mr. Nachmen Leib shouldn't have any complaints about me. I pay lodging fees, I pay interest, and I pay for the house. And I sew for Mr. Nachmen Leib from head to toe. So why should he throw me out of my house, eh?"

"From Nachmen Leib you're expecting fairness? As if he hasn't destroyed enough poor people, the bloodsucker, the usurer!"

"I don't know what you're thinking, Berke! You're laying such a weight on my heart."

Indeed, it was hard on Faivish's heart every time Berke got him talking about the house. A few times, after having one of these conversations with his brother, he made an attempt with Nachmen Leib to get a document in writing.

"I wish nothing but the best for you Mr. Nachmen Leib. A person, you know, is just a person, so maybe, I was thinking . . . If I just had a piece of paper with your signature, you know, as it's done, to show that it's mine."

Nachmen Leib was a tall Jew, built firmly like an oak, with a wide white beard and a meaty red nose with a big wart sitting on top. He would interrupt Faivish's speech in anger, making his red nose even redder.

"Oh so that's how it is? You don't trust me? You want a guarantee from me?"

"God forbid, God forbid," responded Faivish in fear, trying to appease Nachmen and keep him from getting genuinely angry and actually throwing him out of the house. "God forbid. What are you talking about Mr. Nachmen Leib? How could it be that I wouldn't trust you? Who doesn't trust Mr. Nachmen Leib? How could I, Faivish the Tailor, even dare to think of not trusting you? But still, it could be . . ."

"You've pontificated enough." Nachmen Leib would say a bit softer, "I don't want to hear any more of that kind of talk from you. When the right time comes, I will give you a document myself. No one has to remind me. I know what belongs to me and what belongs to someone else. Now, go in peace and depend on me."

After a conversation like that with Nachmen Leib, Faivish would feel relieved enough, and continue to pay every week for the house, interest, and rent. Until one time, when Faivish stopped paying.

Faivish knew nothing of clocks. He woke up at dawn and worked until late at night. When the lamp oil burned out he knew it was time to go to sleep. That's how he worked, year after year, night after night, until one night he got worn out when there was still oil in the lamp. He fell asleep at his work and died with a needle in his hand.

Faivish left a widow and four daughters. Nachmen Leib the Usurer categorically disclaimed Faivish's weekly payments and threw his widow and orphans out of the house.

That's when Berke earned the surname Blizzard. He demolished worlds. Day after day he went to Nachmen Leib's house and hurtled out screams.

"Murderer! Thief! Bloodsucker!" shrieked Berke. "You robbed my brother's widow and their four orphans. But you won't be forgiven! The world is not so forsaken!"

The case came before a rabbinical court. The rabbi ruled that he couldn't determine any definitive evidence that Faivish had indeed paid for the house. And since there was no evidence, and no documents, Nachmen Leib's position held just as much weight as Berke's, especially considering that Berke had never personally witnessed Faivish paying Nachmen Leib.

Nachmen Leib's large house stood in the middle of Market Street. Its windows were always pristinely whitewashed, and its tin roof painted blue. Sturdy oak benches stood on its wide clean porch. In front of the house, several thick acacia trees anchored the picket fencing. In the summer, when the trees were in bloom, their white blossoms shimmered through the green leaves and filled the street with sweet smells. Every afternoon, Nachmen Leib sat on his porch under the trees' shade and observed the bustle of Market Street.

On the other side of the street, across from Nachmen Leib's beautiful house, a collection of market stalls displayed themselves. Rekhl Berke Blizzard's stall stood exactly across from Nachmen Leib's front porch. That's how Berke's hollers earned their reputation in town. As soon as Nachmen Leib appeared on the porch, Berke took to his yelling.

"There he is, the bloodsucker! You'll be punished for working my

"Leech! Bloodsucker! You should get cholera in your bones!" Berke Blizzard cursed Nachmen Leib the Percentnik.

brother to death! Robber! Murderer! Homicidal maniac! You won't be forgiven!" Or he would shriek, "Just look at him, a pillar of the community! He should be sent to Siberia! He sent my brother right into his grave! Leech! Bloodsucker! You should get cholera in your bones!"

The more he cursed Nachmen Leib, the more his voice increased in its rage and shrillness. And he continued to yell like that until Nachmen Leib went back into his house.

The street, and even the whole town, enjoyed how Berke Blizzard was giving the percentnik what he deserved. Even though Berke's voice perforated their brains 'til they could hardly stand it, they found consolation in the fact that somebody was voicing out loud the rage they had felt themselves and was taking on Nachmen Leib's plundering of the town's poor. When Berke called the usurer a thief, a murderer, a bloodsucker, people said it right along with him, some under their breath, some out loud: "You said it, Berke. And how. You give it to him, Berke! Keep at it. Scream for all of us."

2

When Berke was at home in his stooped hut, which, with its patched up, moss-spotted roof, appeared from a distance to be lying on the ground, he never yelled. He was very quiet at home, due to his sense of propriety and his love for his two sons, Khone and Zeidl, and especially for his beautiful and delicate daughter Rivele. Berke noticed, that on account of his bright well-behaved children, the town was beginning to see him as more respectable. Even Mr. Beresh Yechiel, for whom Berke worked as a driver, would ask after his children with great admiration, almost as he would with one of his equals. It was the only thing Mr. Beresh would talk about with Berke, other than his two black horses. Mr. Beresh, the richest man in town, gave Berke a half-ruble bonus every time his wife Rekhl bore him a child.

Rivele's friends called her "Princess" because of her pretty, round, almost babyish face, her delicate skin and rosy cheeks, and the way her parents and brothers guarded and protected her like a jewel. She had dark intelligent eyes, black hair she combed up high on her head, and dressed in fine neat clothing. Rivele could read and write Yiddish, sing well, and she was known in town to be a lovely dancer. Rivele never went out without her brothers as chaperones, whether to a wedding or to the theater when a troupe came to perform. She was courted by the town's best artisans and highest earners.

Khone and Zeidl started working at a very young age. Both of them were short-statured, big-boned, healthy young men, like their father Berke Blizzard. They were good craftsmen and good earners. Khone had quickly become known as one of the best bakers, and Zeidl earned a reputation as a master tailor, in whom the richest customers could entrust their most important projects. Their proficiency in their crafts and their good manners meant both brothers were always employed.

Rivele began to work when she was sixteen years old. Neither her parents nor her brothers wanted her to go to work, but after a lengthy deliberation, it was decided that if she wanted to work, her earnings, together with the weekly contributions from her brothers, and the gifts from her parents, could be put toward her bridal trousseau.

Through the long winter nights, mother and daughter plucked goose and duck feathers.

Every year, Rivele's trousseau grew. Through the long winter nights, mother and daughter sat together plucking soft goose down and duck feathers, and then stuffing them into linen comforters. These blankets made a part of Rivele's bridal trousseau. She collected fine pieces of silk, velvet, and plush. She embroidered the edges of fine towels and the hems of handsome tablecloths, as well as undergarments and handkerchiefs for herself and her intended for their special day.

Over the course of five years, Rivele accrued three full chests, not including the bedding, which lay on the bed and hung all the way to the floor. Her neighbors and friends envied her trousseau, which was worthy even for the daughter of the richest businessman in town.

Rivele was happy with her treasure. Her parents and brothers were also proud to have had a part in the trousseau. Rivele's treasure tied mother, father, brothers and sister ever tighter in their family bond. Rivele and her trousseau became one, united by the silk, velvet, and plush. Rivele's chests stored the hopes and dreams of Berke Blizzard's entire family.

3

Sunday was the town's biggest market day. Peasants streamed into town, some on foot and some in horse-drawn wagons, filling up the stores and shops. From early in the morning until late afternoon, the whole town was consumed with commerce. The peasants sold their produce to the Jews: eggs and flax, pig bristles and chickens, ducks and geese, horses, hides and cows, wheat, corn, oats, and vegetables. Once they had wrapped up their extended bargaining, their calculations, and then counted their money up a few times, then they could start buying. They bought soap and sugar, salt and oil, kerosene, shoes, salted fish, and assorted treats for their children back home—bagels, cookies, candies, whistles, and other novelties—each one according to their means. The better-off peasants could sell horses and wagons, sheep skins and Persian lamb hats, sickles and hoes, sharpening stones, knives, pots, and other supplies for the town's households.

After every Sunday market day, the town would be exhausted from the tumult, haggling, business, and hard work. People looked forward to Sunday all week, and then when the market ended, the shopkeepers caught their breath to go home tired and satisfied.

It happened on one of the Sunday market days. The day had already ended, but the setting sun still burned a bit between the roofs. The peasants had already departed. The bustle had been cut off, as if by a knife, and the town was quiet, like a mill after it stopped grinding. Here and there a tarrying peasant rushed to complete a last meager purchase. The shopkeepers were done trying. They had become too worn out to bargain over price. A little more for this customer, a little less for that one—it wasn't really going to make a difference at this point. The stalls with bagels, cookies, and candies, which stood all along Market Street, looked abandoned. The women who worked the stalls had been wanting to pack up their leftover stock and go home for a long time already. They were all just waiting for one of them to go first.

All of a sudden a wild scream took over the entirety of Market Street. Berke Blizzard ran across the street and yelled as if possessed, "Help!

Robbed! Fleeced like a sheep! Dammit somebody robbed us! Goddammit! Rivele!"

Shopkeepers ran out of their stores. Heads poked out of windows. Everyone was used to Berke Blizzard's yelling, but Market Street had never heard this kind of insane screaming, not even from him.

Berke paused next to his wife Rekhl's stall, panting, but continuing to scream in alarm. The other vendor-women gathered around Rekhl's stall, along with shopkeepers, passersby, and people who had come out of their houses. Rekhl was distraught. Barely catching his breath and with his eyes popping out of his head, Berke screeched out the great misfortune with ripped up words. "Robbed . . . We've been robbed . . . Someone stole Rivele's—Rivele's trousseau."

"Oh no! Good God!" Rekhl wrung her hands. Her slender, weak body shuddered. She fainted into Berke's arms.

"Help! Save her! A doctor!" yelled Berke.

The vendor-women took Rekhl from Berke's arms with trembling hands, sat her on a bench, and washed her gaunt face with cold water. They tenderly slapped her thinned-out cheeks and squeezed lemon juice into her mouth.

Berke and Rekhl's disaster became a uniting misfortune for the street, the entire community, and the whole town.

"Rivele's trousseau has been completely stolen . . . It's terrible! The robbers should suffer! Oh what a pity . . ."

The news soon reached Khone, Zeidl, and Rivele, and they learned of the misfortune. Rivele went pale and stood beside her mother, quietly sobbing with overflowing eyes. Khone and Zeidl stood apart from the crowd with a group of their young baker and tailor friends speaking quietly and rapidly.

"Rivele," Khone called out to his sister.

Rivele came over to the circle of her brothers and their friends, who gave her a quick nod.

"Rivele," Khone turned to his sister, looking pale and upset, "when was the last time you saw Bentshik the Thief?"

"Yesterday," whimpered Rivele.

"Did you speak with him?" asked Khone.

Rivele got embarrassed. She glanced quickly at Khone, Zeidl, their friends, and then lowered her eyes and tearfully explained that Bentshik regularly waited for her when she came home from work, and that he spoke of love and how he wanted to marry her.

Khone, Zeidl, and their friends left. They went into the bakery where Khone worked. Each of them armed himself with a thick piece of wood, and they all set out to find Bentshik the Thief. They looked for him in every bar, every inn, every seedy place in town. But no dice. They searched all night, in the houses of each of his friends and relatives, but couldn't find a trace of him. No one knew where he had gone. At dawn, they headed home exhausted. It was as if Bentshik the Thief had disappeared into thin air. It only firmed up their certainty that he had stolen Rivele's trousseau to punish her for avoiding him and not wanting to marry him.

Khone and Zeidl stopped going to work. They searched for Bentshik every day and night. They scoped every house Bentshik used for a hideout. The workers' association called a meeting at which they voted to instate a special committee to support Khone and Zeidl in looking for the thief. The association also decided to expel Bentshik from town, but first he would have to return Rivele's trousseau.

Rivele fell ill from the strain and had to stay in bed. Rekhl tended to her beloved daughter, who had become so broken in just one day that it was hard to recognize her. Berke sighed in the stillness. A heavy sorrow enveloped the entire household.

4

Bentshik, the son of Zalmen the Black, was hiding out in one of the peasant huts near the woods outside the city, waiting for things to cool off in town. His steady pal and right-hand man Shaike Ox was with him. Shaike was a tall, healthy young man, so strong that he had become the second in command of the town's gang of thieves.

Motke Telegraph, the gang's spy, came to Bentshik each night to bring him news from town, along with food, brandy, and wine for Bentshik and Shaike.

Motke Telegraph was the gang's Bureau of Information. He was a thin little guy with a pointy face, long pointy nose, and nervous dark, darting eyes. Motke went around town silently, just looking, watching, and listening. He had his own methods of finding out who had money or jewelry and which fabric shops had large stocks of expensive materials. Then Motke Telegraph delivered all the dope to Bentshik, who figured out the rest.

Motke knew who in the gang had a loose tongue. He kept an eye on the little rascals who busied themselves with petty thefts. If any of them showed some talent, Motke would recommend him for Bentshik's gang.

After they had pulled off a big heist, Bentshik and his men went to hide out in one of their spots. Motke would go around town to sniff out where things stood. Until he gave the signal that things had eased up, none of the thieves risked setting foot out of their hideout. It was bad news for anyone who dared sneak out without Motke's permission. Shaike Ox, or once in a while even Bentshik himself, would beat him to a pulp and dock his share of the take. Bentshik's order was that no one in the gang could disobey Motke's ruling, and Bentshik's order was law.

Bentshik had just turned twenty-five years old. He had grown into a tall man with a well-muscled, energetic, flexible body. He had a smooth, handsome face, a nicely carved nose, strong white teeth, and a confident chin. His straight black hair paired well with his large, black, glowing eyes. He was always neatly dressed and appeared more like a traveling salesman from an established business than like the leader of a thieves' gang. He had survived the years of bloody fights it took for him to conquer the earlier gang leaders and become the new chief, without getting so much as a scratch on his face. All his head wounds had healed up and any marks were covered over by his full, thick hair.

When he was fifteen, Bentshik and his baby sister had become completely orphaned. Their father, Zalmen the Black, a tall energetic guy, ran a tough racket. He dealt in horses, and, due to his poverty, didn't dig into whether the horses were so "kosher." In fact, Zalmen and his childhood friend and partner Abish the Bear dealt mostly in stolen horses. Zalmen was beaten to death in a fight with peasants who recognized their stolen horses, and Abish the Bear was so gravely injured that he was laid up in the hospital for six months. His great strength was all that kept him alive. After Zalmen's horrible death, his wife Soreh fell ill from the heartbreak and died two months after her husband. Bentshik and his little sister Tsipke were left at sea. Zalmen's sister from the neighboring town took in Tsipke. Abish and his wife Freidl took in Bentshik. But Bentshik didn't stay long at his new parents' home. He ran away soon after, and it was as if he had disappeared underwater. Abish looked for him and even spent money on the search. Occasionally, he heard troubling rumors about Bentshik. One time he even heard that Bentshik had been sent to jail somewhere very far away. So Abish went to the town lawyer, who asked around in higher places, but they never received any details.

A few years later, Bentshik suddenly turned up in town. No one knew where from. He was unrecognizable. He was a full-grown adult, walking around sharply dressed, checking out the town and spending money on himself everywhere he went. Abish understood that Bentshik was a lost cause and avoided him. Bentshik stayed in town and, through bitter fights, took over the gang leadership.

Bentshik carried out most of his robberies in the poor surrounding villages, but he did some work in his own town when it promised a worthwhile payout. No one in the gang would even think about pinching someone in their own town without Bentshik's permission. And no thief from any other town dared stick his nose into Bentshik's territory. So you could say he "protected" the town from other thieves. When he did do a bit of work in his own town, it would be a juicy bite on a rich man's tab. That's how Bentshik and the city got along peacefully. The residents feared him and his gang, and he didn't seek out any extra conflicts. He came to enjoy people being afraid of him. Once in a while, it even occurred to him that the town looked at him with great esteem, and it pleased him.

Bentshik's love for Rivele blazed from the first day he saw her. He promised himself he would marry her. He started courting her with that intention in mind. He awaited her on the back streets she took to walk home from work, and asked her to marry him. He spoke to her of love and told her there was no one more beautiful in the whole world.

At first, Rivele liked those encounters with Bentshik. She liked having the strong, good-looking man, who made the whole town tremble in fear, asking to be her husband. A few times, she even let herself request and accept gifts from him, once a golden watch, another time a bracelet with tiny diamonds, a diamond pin, and other little pieces of jewelry. Bentshik swore to Rivele, on the honor of his deceased mother and father, that he would give up his shady dealings once and for all and start over with a decent, honorable lifestyle, if only she would marry him. He promised to cover her in diamonds and pearls from head to toe and set her up in a life of luxury, like a genuine princess with maids and servants, because he had already saved up enough. He was a very rich man.

Rivele told him it couldn't be. She already had an intended groom and wasn't going to call off the match. Bentshik asked her to run away with him to America.

Rivele came to fear Bentshik and told her brothers about him. They didn't take the whole story seriously. But in any case, they decided that one of them would walk Rivele home from work for one week, and then the other brother would walk her home the next week. Bentshik observed from afar how one of her brothers waited for Rivele every evening, and he understood it was because of him. His desire for thievery began to seethe. He became even more enraged when he learned that Rivele would soon become a bride, that she was about to get engaged to Abish the Bear's only son, the bright and good-looking Avreml, the best wood-carver in town. He received that news from Motke the Spy. Bentshik waited for a chance when Rivele happened to be walking home alone and went to intimidate her, warning that he would take revenge.

He spoke to her of love and said there is no one more beautiful in the whole world.

"If I don't have you, no one will have you," said Bentshik.

The next day, he stole Rivele's trousseau. He had worked out a whole plan to overwhelm Rivele so completely that she would fall to her knees and beg him to marry her. He swore that even if it cost him his life, he must carry out his plan and wed the princess.

5

A heavy gloom set in at Abish the Bear's house soon after. Freidl and Abish didn't sleep a wink at all that whole Sunday night. They felt for Rivele. They loved her and thought of her as their future daughter-in-law. They couldn't have dreamed of a better match for their Avreml. They knew how dear and beloved Rivele was to their only child. And they loved Rivele like their own daughter. Their house had brightened when Rivele and Avreml used to come in on Saturday nights after their walk. Freidl would treat her to their best hospitality. She would dust off Rivele's chair, and when her Avreml walked Rivele home, Freidl would stand at the threshold of the open door glowing and feeling fortunate, following both of the children with her eyes until they disappeared in the distance.

Avreml had grown tall and straight like an arrow, just like his mother. His gentle blue eyes shone from his round face with a tender goodness. He had curly dark-blond hair that bordered his brow like a crown. The whole town loved him: the ladies for his beauty, and the leaders for his calm, his courtesy, and his devotion to his parents. For Freidl and Abish, Avreml was their entire joy in life, God's reward for their repentance from the sins they had committed in their younger years. Avreml was an artist of a wood-carver, never missing a day of work and earning enough to outfit himself well, buy valuable gifts for his beloved Rivele, and save up a bit of money in order to open a workshop of his own.

Sunday night, when Rivele was sick from the stress of the theft, Avreml didn't come home. That was the first night in his twenty-three years he didn't sleep at home. He sat beside Rivele's bed until late in the night. Afterward, he wandered the streets without a direction, not knowing himself where he was going. His head was spinning between his ill and suffering Rivele, her trousseau, which she had labored over for five whole years, and Bentshik the Thief, who had stolen the trousseau. He didn't know what to do, but he did feel that he had to do something to help Rivele. A few times, not understanding how it had happened, he suddenly noticed that he was standing in front of Rivele's house. Lamp-light shone weakly through the small windows. He could tell Berke's household wasn't asleep. He felt bad for Berke, for Rekhl, such a fine person, for Rivele, and for her brothers. He wanted to go ahead and open the door, but for some reason he didn't dare go into Rivele's in the middle of the night, so he set off again wandering the streets. He got home before dawn. He went into his room quietly, drew the curtains over the windows, shoved off his shoes, dragged off his coat, and, still wearing his pants, threw himself on his bed, which his mother prepared for him with white sheets each night.

When Avreml woke, the sun was already shining through the windows into his room. He stayed lying in bed. His mind was still tangled up with the same gloomy thoughts as the previous night. He wanted to run to Rivele, but he remained spread out in bed. Freidl came into his room with soft steps. Avreml recognized her footsteps. He continued lying in the same pose.

"Good morning, son." Freidl greeted Avreml with measured tenderness, and, without waiting for an answer, called him to breakfast.

Avreml responded in a sad voice that he wasn't hungry. Freidl asked how Rivele was doing. Avreml answered briefly and harshly.

"Sick."

"Are you not going to work today?" asked Freidl.

"No."

His mother exited the room with the same soft steps as she had entered.

Abish was sitting in the large dining room, at the round table encircled with chairs, with a half-drunk glass of tea, his arms wrapped around his barrel chest, sunk in thought. He could feel some sort of calamity creeping up on him. He didn't know where this calamity would come from, but he was certain that this episode with Rivele's trousseau wouldn't be resolved easily.

Memories from long ago knocked around in his head. He was reminded of the time, just after his wedding, when he had been sentenced for theft to a one-year imprisonment. His Freidl had just become pregnant with Avreml. As if it were yesterday, he could see Freidl accompanying him with her tear-filled blue eyes. He remembered how, when he got out of prison, Avreml was already four-months old. His friend Zalmen the Black took him on as a partner in his horse business. They had made an agreement with each other not to deal with any un-kosher merchandise. But poverty harassed them both, and they gave into their impious impulses. The partners began earning. The business grew steadily, and it all could have gone fine. If it weren't for Orke the Snitch, they both would have been rich men. Orke ratted them out, and his friend Zalmen was sent off to prison.

Abish remembered each wicked winter night. He sat at home pouring glass after glass of liquor. It burned him up that his friend had been put away. He filled up with rage against Orke the Snitch. All of a sudden, he jumped out of his chair like a snake had bitten him and went right for the door. Freidl blocked his way. Avreml was already ten years old, growing well and beaming like the sun. Freidl shouted, "You're not going Abish! You've got a murderous look burning in your eyes. I'm scared something terrible is going to happen."

But Abish pushed her away, opened the door, and ran off for the snitch. Orke was sitting and eating heartily. Abish grabbed him in one hand, and with the other started hammering on Orke's head until he collapsed to the ground like a felled tree. Orke was dead. Abish was sent to Siberia for seven years.

Abish didn't want to think about that bitter time in Siberia. When he came home, Freidl took him back just as if nothing had happened. For those seven years she had wandered about among strangers, working as a servant, and enduring immeasurable degradations. It pierced his heart. He felt awful that he had caused so much suffering for his good-hearted Freidl. In that time, Avreml had grown up and started apprenticing with Shabsi the wood-carver.

Zalmen, who had already been released for a long while, took Abish back into their partnership. Soon after, the calamity occurred. The peasants beat Zalmen to death, and he himself lay in the hospital for months.

When he got out of the hospital, he made a promise to himself, and swore to his Freidl, that his hand would never again touch un-kosher merchandise. He submitted to Freidl and went off to the rabbi to swear an official vow that he would become an honest man, just like all the other honest men. Abish remembered how they guided him in the synagogue, just like they would have guided a bar-mitsveh boy. He stood in front of the open ark, wrapped in a talis, with a minyen of Jews standing by him. Two large lights shone from the lecterns next to the open ark. The rabbi, small, mild-mannered Rebbe Shimele, spoke the words, and he repeated them one by one. Abish broke out in a cold sweat when he reminded himself of his vow. He remembered how the rabbi shook his hand and wished him success. The synagogue Jews also shook his hand and wished him an honest, easy life. He left the synagogue with a light heart, feeling clean and filled with a new hope. The outside air lifted his spirits. The town became even dearer and more of a home to him.

From that time on, he stayed away from un-kosher merchandise. Easy earnings didn't tempt him anymore. He was satisfied with a scant piece of kosher bread. And now, he suddenly felt that he was standing at the threshold of a great new test. Abish hadn't noticed that Freidl was in the room. He hadn't heard her sit down in a chair next to him. She called his name. With a start, Abish spun his large head, which was covered in black and gray hair down his neck, and rumbled, "Huh? Did you say something Freidl?"

He looked at her and felt his heart ache. Freidl was dark as dirt. Her eyes were filled with tears.

"Abish," she said in a shaky voice, "Avreml hasn't eaten anything. He's sitting alone and pouring liquor into himself."

Abish's heavy body rocked. He took his hands out of his breast pockets and stretched his forearms out on the table.

"Liquor?" he repeated back to Freidl, and without waiting for an answer said to himself, "How did Avreml come to start drinking liquor?" A deep sigh ripped out of Abish's chest. His large head, with its wide beard, lay on his strong hands.

"Abish," cried out Freidl, "why are you silent? This is a calamity, I'm telling you, Avreml is in a bad state."

He lifted his head and looked at Freidl. She leaned toward him, wiped her eyes with her apron, and said in a hard, cold tone, "Abish, a murderous look is burning in his eyes . . ."

Abish got up from his chair and bellowed, "Freidl!"

His right hand lifted in the air. Freidl shifted her head and covered her face with both her hands. Abish's hand stayed in the air for a moment, as if it were frozen, and then slowly lowered. He held onto the table so as not to fall. His legs wobbled. With difficulty, he set himself back down on the chair. A dead silence took over the house. It seemed like even the large clock on the wall had stopped ticking. Finally, Abish quietly groaned, "Oy Freidl, something terrible is happening to us! A calamity!"

Freidl didn't answer. She felt awful for her Abish, but she also felt relief in her heart and a warmth inside. A great happiness filled each of her limbs, like the first time she had felt Avreml's little mouth suckling her breast. It gave her great satisfaction that Abish had overcome his wild anger and not struck her, as he had in years past. Since the time Abish had made his vow, she hadn't stopped worrying that a great anger might overtake him and he would return to his old behaviors. Now, she was certain that her Abish would stay pure once and for all, a decent man, the equal of all other decent men. Her fear disappeared in that instant. She was sure that he was saved, and that the Abish of old didn't exist anymore, that he would never return. She also believed that her husband would finally do something about Rivele and Avreml and about the robbery.

In her new calm, Freidl let out a sigh.

Abish lifted himself up out of the chair through his exhaustion, and turned to go into the side room to Avreml. Freidl followed him with quiet steps. He opened the door of his son's room and stood silently at the threshold. Freidl stood behind him. The smell of strong liquor slammed out of the room. An almost empty white bottle of liquor with an empty glass stood on the four-cornered table. Avreml was sitting at the table, his head lying on his right arm. His left hand was holding the empty glass. When he noticed his father, he tried to get up, but his feet didn't serve him and he almost fell. Abish rushed into the room and caught his son in his powerful arms. Avreml felt better instantly. His head, which had felt full of lead, fell on Abish's breast under his wide beard. He cried like a child, "Papa, Papa, help me! Rivele is so sick."

Abish's heart tightened. He felt for his only son. With his big hairy hand, he stroked his son's messy curly hair. He said, "Don't you worry my child, God will help."

Two big tears shone in Abish's eyes, rolled down over his beard, and fell on Avreml's curly hair.

Freidl couldn't believe her own eyes. For the first time since she met her husband, she saw him crying. That, as well as the great pain she felt for her son, was enough to set her crying, too. She knew she was crying mixed tears, from the calamity, but also from pride. She helped Abish get Avreml into bed and take off his shoes. When Abish had left his son's little room, he stroked his beard with both hands, looked outside through the window, paced the entire large dining room a few times with measured steps, and said quietly to himself, "Don't rush yourself Abish. Nothing good comes from rushing."

He felt calmer. There was an ease in all his limbs, and he could sense his former strength throughout his body. It had been a long while since he had felt like this. He could still feel the warmth from his son's face on his breast.

"Avremele my child, your papa will help," Abish mumbled to himself. "Freidl," he called to his wife, "you got anything good to eat?"

Freidl heard his call through the open door of Avreml's room and smiled broadly. She knew what that signaled.

"Soon, Abish," she called back, "soon I'll get the table ready."

6

Abish got up early the next morning. He had slept well, like he always did the night before a big job. He ate bread with herring for breakfast and drank several glasses of tea. He knew Avreml hadn't gone to work. Freidl told him that he had gone over to Rivele's and that he had calmed down.

Abish didn't say anything about it. He put on his Shabbos suit, combed his beard, and headed for the door. When he reached the doorway and put his hand on the doorknob, he turned his head to his wife and said, "Don't wait for me to eat supper. I may be late."

Freidl didn't ask where he was going or when he would be home. She remembered too well from all those years, that in times like this you don't talk too much, and you don't ask questions.

"Go, go. Take care, and come home safe," she wished her husband.

Abish gave the mezuzeh a kiss and closed the door behind him.

He surveyed all the backstreets of the town, strolling slowly and easily, as if nothing were wrong. Here and there he ran into an acquaintance, greeted them with a nod, and kept on walking. Abish didn't want to get involved in a conversation with anyone. He was looking for Motke the Spy. When he found one of Motke's friends, he asked whether they knew where he could find Motke. If they didn't know, Abish cut the conversation short and continued on his way. Those backstreets, which he hadn't walked for a long time, were strangely familiar to him, and at the same time, foreign. The buildings seemed shorter and the streets narrower. Everything had somehow become shrunken, and he felt the alleys pressing in on him. Even the great wide square, which had an endless number of small passageways on all its sides leading to the horse market and to all the market streets, seemed to him like they had become smaller and narrower.

From a distance, Abish recognized an old associate of his, who he knew to be involved with the established thieves, as well as the up-and-coming ones. He slowed his step.

When they met, they greeted each other warmly, like brothers.

"Well would you look at that, it's Leizer. You haven't changed a bit.

Y'don't even look a day older," Abish said to his former friend with contrived warmth.

"And you, Abish, why, you look younger and sprier than ever. Seems like once you leave this dirty racket, you get to go right to the Garden of Eden . . . Do you miss it now Abish?"

Leizer gave his little red beard a pat and looked Abish in the eyes, like he was looking to read some truth in them.

Abish laughed. "How could I not miss it? So many years with such a good band of brothers. You don't forget a thing like that. It's got a pull y'know?"

Leizer felt flattered by the speech. Abish registered it and offered, "You should come over some time. You're an old pal after all. You know, Leizer," Abish stretched his words, "I would bring you home right now, but I'm in the middle of something. I've got a bit of a job to do that I shouldn't put off."

Leizer scoped Abish out suspiciously with his gray eyes.

"What are you talkin' about Abish? You miss your old easy money with its troubles and tribulations?"

Abish smiled and gave him a brotherly shove with his elbow.

"Troubles," he said, "are just what I'm trying to avoid. No one has to seek out troubles. They come over to your house on their own, and sometimes they get brought packed full in chests. Do you get me Leizer? Or do I have to spell it out for you?"

Leizer perked up. He squinted his eyes and asked, "When's this chest coming Abish? Is it something major?"

"You can be sure, Leizer, that Abish doesn't forget a brother from the old days. But now, I've got to meet up with Bentshik. Do you know maybe where he's holed up?"

Leizer's imagination heated up. He was thinking about the chests and wanted to be sure he wouldn't be left out.

"Abish," he said, "Bentshik can't sneak out now, and no one can visit him. He must be somewhere in one of the old hideouts. Pop over to Shimke, you'll find Motke there, and you can lay out all your cards to him. And keep me in mind, Abish. I'm your old pal after all, and you know I still don't have a penny to my name."

"Don't you worry, Leizer," interrupted Abish, "It's gonna be alright. But keep it quiet."

Abish wasn't strolling anymore. He knew where he was going and he set off decisively to Motke's brother Shimke's place.

He stopped walking when he got to the house that stood on its own, a bit isolated from the other houses. It was the only house on the little street that had its own plastered sidewalk and two large trees near its front window. The front of the house was whitewashed, and the window frames and door were painted red with fresh paint. A long narrow bench stood exactly as Abish remembered it, under the shade of the tree on the right side of the house. That was Shimke's wine bar, where shady characters drank and ate. No respectable gentleman from town had ever set foot there.

Abish opened the door and entered the long narrow corridor. On one side of the corridor were several doors. On the other side there were only two. They led into the great room where only important guests fraternized. Abish opened one of the doors to that room. A long wide table, surrounded by chairs, stood in the middle of the room. Smaller tables stood by the walls. Motke the Spy and his brother Shimke were sitting at the edge of the large table playing cards.

Shimke got up from his chair and shouted, "Oh ho, would you just look who's come for a visit!" He turned out one of the chairs and invited Abish to sit.

Abish took a seat and said chummily, "Just like old times almost."

Shimke left the room for barely a minute. Shimke's wife came in shortly after and set out a large bottle of red wine with glasses on the table. She left and came right back, setting fried chicken, stuffed chicken necks, pickles, and bread alongside them. Having finished her work, she vanished from the room.

Motke sat silently and didn't move. It hadn't taken him long to figure out why Abish the Bear had suddenly shown up at his brother's wine bar. He waited to see what would happen. He had heard a lot about Abish, from when Abish was younger, and he held him in high respect, chiefly due to how Abish had settled up with Orke the Snitch on account of his friend and partner Zalmen.

Shimke filled the glasses and invited Abish to taste his wine.

"You're also an expert in wine aren't you?" Shimke asked Abish with a smile.

The whole time, Abish hadn't even looked at Motke so much as once, even though he could feel that Motke wasn't taking his eyes off of him. He took a sip of wine from the glass, gave a cluck of his tongue, and declared his expert opinion, "A solid glass of wine. It's already five or six years old, eh?" He slowly slurped the glass of wine.

Shimke quickly refilled his glass and said, "Abish, you're not going to insult my Braindl's roast chicken are you?"

Abish got serious and answered, "Abish has never insulted anyone in his life." He glanced at Motke with his big eyes and asked Shimke, "That's your little brother, eh?"

"Yeah," Shimke answered and added, "He's already a big shot on his own."

Abish set in on the roast chicken. He promptly ate a sizable portion and got right to the point.

"You want to know what I'm doing here, Shimke, on an ordinary Tuesday?"

Shimke focused his large ears, although he already knew Abish was going to talk about Rivele's trousseau, and answered, "Whenever you want to come over, you're always a welcome guest."

Abish interrupted his speech, "I want to ask you, as an old friend, to let Bentshik know I want to see him."

Shimke lost his bearings. He hadn't expected such an open and explicit request. He looked at Motke. Motke's little eyes were doing a nervous dance.

"You know," continued Abish, "I'm asking you to do this as a favor to me. Someday I'll pay you back, not that I want you to be in need of it."

He took out his wooden tobacco box, rolled a thick cigarette, lit it, took in a puff, and let out a cloud of smoke. He looked Shimke in the eyes. Abish's piercing gaze unnerved Shimke.

"Abish," Shimke said softly, "Bentshik hasn't been around here for a long time already. I don't even know if he's in town."

Abish jumped right in while he was still talking, "Meaning, you don't want to do me this favor. If you did, you would make Motke here, when he brings this roast chicken to Bentshik, tell him I want to see him."

Shimke and Motke sat still like they were dumbstruck. For Shimke, the conversation had gotten too hot. Motke got in the mix.

"Who told you about that?"

"A little birdy," Abish said curtly, intensely, and with a smile.

"So why don't you ask your little birdy where Bentshik is?" asked Motke, greatly satisfied with how cleverly he was sparring with Abish.

"Oh, you sure are a smart young man," said Abish and turned to Motke. "So I'll spill the secret that my birdy is hiding out under the eaves of that peasant's straw hut where Bentshik the big shot is laying low waiting for the heat to cool off."

"Oh, what a smart birdy," uttered Motke, turning pale.

"So here's what's gonna happen," said Abish to Motke, looking right into his beady eyes. "You'll say that Abish wants to see him. I want to see him at my house. At my house nothing bad will happen to him. I want things to turn out well for him, and if you think about it, Motke," Abish stretched out these last words while holding his broad thick beard, "I figure that's how things will turn out well for you, too. Do I make myself clear?" he asked Shimke, who sat shaken and shocked.

Neither he nor Motke could understand how Abish knew about Bentshik's hideout.

"But Reb Abish." Shimke gathered up his strength. "I've got to ask, what does this have to do with my brother Motye?"[1]

Abish laughed out loud. His large heavy body shook. He got up from his seat, put his tobacco box, which had been laying on the table, back in his pocket, gave his pocket a light pat and said, "OK, thanks, Shimke, for your wine and for your tasty cooking. And you Motke, tell Bentshik that I'll keep good wine and good roast chicken and duck ready for him, and that I'll expect him tomorrow, or the day after tomorrow, whichever he wants. If you want, you can come, too. With Abish, it's better to drink with him than to fight with him. Whaddya say, Shimke? You know Abish better than this kid. Have a good one."

He went out to the street and set off for home at a clip. Now he was struck with a wild rage against Bentshik, against Motke, and against

---

1 Motye is his more formal given name, while Motke is a nickname.

Shimke. He gnashed his strong teeth. "What a fleabag, that Motke," he said to himself. "What a way to run things." He pressed his steely hands into fists, then stopped himself and got an urge to go back to Shimke. "I should have crushed that little flea when I had the chance," he said to himself and headed home. He was certain that Motke would tell Bentshik about their conversation. *There's no telling yet what would come of it. There's still time. Just don't rush it . . .*

7

When it had gotten dark, Motke headed out to Bentshik and told Shaike and the rest of them that things had quieted off in town, but that he didn't like how Abish the Bear was butting in. He filled them in on his chat with Abish and didn't leave out any particulars. He spoke over-excitedly about old Abish: his giant strength, his savvy, and his calm. "He's a tough guy if ever there was one," he said in awe.

Bentshik chuckled. "It's working out even better than I figured it."

Motke turned his peepers on him.

"I'd already made up my mind," Bentshik let him know, "to meet with Abish and with Avreml as soon as things cooled off in town, to tell both of them that no one creeps into Bentshik's garden. But this is even better. Abish invited me himself."

"Wouldn't it be better to catch Avreml when he's coming from work and tell him what's what?" suggested Motke. "Old Abish is a bad-tempered guy, a real bear."

Bentshik smiled and Shaike Ox laughed out loud.

"Motke's scared of an old bear," teased Shaike. "I'll bring you his pelt, and you can sew yourself a fur coat."

"Don't forget Shaike, bears love ox meat," Motke shot back.

Bentshik cut them off. "Motke, you sleep here tonight. Tomorrow we'll sample Abish's wine. And if he does want to get tough with us, we'll snack on some bear meat."

Shaike liked Bentshik's joke. Motke was silent. He didn't dare mutiny against Bentshik, but he was certain the plan wasn't going to work, and he asked Bentshik, "Wouldn't it be easier to put off the visit to Abish until later?"

"No," answered Bentshik. "I don't want Abish to think I'm scared of him. And it will be easier the sooner we knock out any notion Abish might have of messing around anymore in other peoples' business. If we wait too long, Abish could do something else stupid."

Motke could see that Bentshik was right, but he still felt the idea of going to Abish's wasn't going to turn out well. Only after Bentshik

Motke Telegraph, the gang's spy, and Shaike Ox plan a little job.

reassured him that it was going to be a short, quiet visit, did Motke sign on to the plan.

When Abish got home, the sun was already starting to set. Freidl had been waiting for him silently agitated. Avreml was at Rivele's.

"Put on the samovar," he ordered, and went to wash his hands.

Drinking his tea, he told Freidl to prepare fried chicken, duck, and wine. "We might have company tomorrow."

Freidl didn't ask him who or why. That evening, and until late at night, she was busy preparing for the guests. At dawn, she was ready to do the frying. She worked hard so everything looked nice and the food turned out delicious. She arranged the livers and gizzards and stuffed necks, all on separate plates, and the chicken and duck separately, too. She sliced bread, prepared a big dish of pickles, and glasses of red wine. Everything was set on the kitchen table, which was covered with a clean white tablecloth. The house smelled of fried garlic and pepper.

Abish sat in the house and smoked fat cigarettes he rolled himself. Avreml was at work. The morning passed. No one came. Freidl got a little nervous. The afternoon passed. No one came. Abish sat and smoked. Freidl couldn't find a place to settle in. She tried lying down a few times, but as soon as she dozed off, she woke up suddenly. She thought she heard someone coming. She kept looking at the large alarm clock. Abish was quiet and she didn't ask him anything. She was accustomed to it.

Outside dimmed. The evening stretched long and black like tar. All of a sudden, the door opened. Bentshik, Motke, and Shaike came into the house. Freidl became shaky. She lost her breath. For a moment, she forgot who Bentshik really was. Hovering before her eyes, she saw the faces of Soreh and Zalmen the Black, Bentshik's parents, who had also been her good friends. She remembered how she had told Soreh on her deathbed that she would take Bentshik in and take care of him like a mother. Freidl wanted to embrace the large, strong Bentshik and press him to her hurting heart. Tears filled her eyes.

"Freidl, what are you just standing there for?"

Abish's voice brought her back to the brutal reality. The guests sat down around the table. Abish sat himself next to Bentshik. Freidl served the food. She still felt scrambled up. She heard that the men were speaking, but she didn't catch the words. When everything was set on the table, she sat on the side and sunk her eyes in Bentshik's face. She couldn't make up her mind about whether he looked like his mother or not. Yes, his bearing, his strength, and his black hair, he inherited from his father, Zalmen the Black. But his fine face reminded her of Soreh. Even so, an odd hardness and arrogance around his mouth had displaced his mother's goodness, which had poured from her face. Freidl had completely forgotten about the robbery, and she wasn't interested in the conversation the men were quietly conducting among themselves. Zalmen, Soreh, and Bentshik coursed together in her mind and it seemed to her that Zalmen and Soreh were sitting at the table and Bentshik was sitting between them. A sweet happiness embraced her and she smiled with a deep contentment.

The door opened. Avreml halted, standing at the doorway like he had turned to stone, his eyes wide open, staring at the guests. Freidl jumped up from her seat. She immediately caught on to what was afoot.

"Hey, Avreml," called out Bentshik in fake friendliness, "what are you standing like a stone at the door for? Have a seat here at the table. Are you still shy in front of people? You're a big boy already."

Avreml walked to the table with measured steps and sat down next to his father. Bentshik poured him a glass of wine and said, "Can you drink a glass of wine yet, or do you still chew raisins?"

Shaike Ox laughed. Motke the Spy didn't take his eyes off Avreml. Now he understood why Rivele had fallen for Avreml and run away from Bentshik.

"Nu, so show us how you drink up a glass of wine," Bentshik continued taunting Avreml.

Abish was silent. Avreml took a glass of wine in his hand, calmly raised it in the air, said, "L'chaim," and swallowed it down like water.

"Alright, you really are a big boy now! Drink another," said Bentshik, refilling Avreml's emptied glass.

Avreml emptied the glass again and asked Bentshik, "Did you bring Rivele's things?"

Bentshik and Shaike laughed out loud.

"What are you?" teased Bentshik, "Rivele's lawyer?"

"I'm Rivele's fiancé," he answered firm and calm. "Rivele is sick with heartache. I want you to give me back Rivele's trousseau."

Shaike Ox barked out another laugh. His red face reddened even more.

"You don't say," said Bentshik, also in a calm tone, although little flames had lit up in his eyes, and his face had gone white. "So, you want Rivele's things. And if you don't get them?"

Abish smiled and thought to himself, *God almighty have mercy on him if he raises a hand to Avreml.* Motke saw Abish's smile and his mouth started to dry out. His little eyes darted from Abish to Bentshik and from Bentshik to Avreml. He wanted to put an end to this visit, but he didn't know how. For the first time, he didn't have any ideas. He felt sore at Bentshik for bringing them to Abish's and he started thinking about clearing out and saving his own hide.

"So whaddya say Avreml," Bentshik continued questioning, "what are you going to do if I won't give you Rivele's things?"

Avreml blanched. Freidl saw it and bit her lips. Avreml poured himself another glass of wine and drank it down in one gulp. Then he calmly wiped his mouth. Everyone was silent. Now he answered Bentshik's question. He answered it softly and with restraint, "If you want to remain alive, you will return Rivele's things to me."

Bentshik let out a long, quiet whistle. Shaike Ox, who hadn't paused from stuffing himself with the tasty fried chicken and slurping the wine, butted in and said with an idiotic laugh, "Bentshik, it looks to me like we're going to have to lay Avreml on a knee and give him a good spanking to teach him how he's gotta show respect to his elders."

Abish folded his arms across his chest, looked at Shaike Ox, and smiled calmly. He thought, *If he touches Avreml with one finger, God almighty have mercy on him.* He was just waiting for a good excuse so he could be left with a clean conscience. He wanted one of these thieves to raise a hand. Motke didn't take his eyes off Abish. His calm and his smile unnerved him. He started feeling genuinely afraid of the old giant.

"Bentshik," began Abish suddenly, "I'm your friend. I was your papa's best friend." He twirled a thick cigarette, took a drag, and let out a cloud of smoke from his mouth. "Me and your pop were like brothers, and my Freidl and your mom were like sisters. Whenever things got hot, I always took the rap and got locked up to save your pa. When Orke the Snitch got your pop sent away, I stepped up for him and got packed off again. I went through the fire for your father. I haven't even treated my own wife and children as loyally as I did your pop. I saved him from death more than once. That last time, when the tragedy happened, I would have saved him then, too. I stuck out my neck and yelled with all my might: 'Zalmen, run, save yourself!' I wish he would have listened to me. But nothing doing. That's just how it worked out. And you know the rest, Bentshik. I took you in. You were just like my own son. But you ran away to God knows where. I searched and searched. I wanted you back. It hurt me as much as it would have for my own flesh and blood. And now I'm asking you a favor. You get me Bentshik? I, Abish, your father's friend, am begging you. Don't embarrass me. I don't deserve that from you," Abish finished. The house was quiet. Bentshik lowered his head.

"So what do you say Bentshik?" Abish asked quietly.

Bentshik took a smoke. He turned in his chair toward Abish and said, "It's easy for you to talk. Just think about it: I've got no father, no mother, no sisters, no brothers; I grew up like a dog, tramping from clink to clink. So what, Abish? Am I really a dog? I don't get anything in this world, huh? Avreml gets everything, and I get nothing?"

Freidl wiped her eyes.

"But Bentshik," said Abish, "she doesn't want you, she wants Avreml. So I ask you, what good is going to come from forcing her? And if you don't give back her things, how does that make anything better? She's still not going to want you."

"Who says she doesn't want me?" Bentshik flared up. "I know better. It's just that Avreml butted in. I'm telling you, he's playing with fire."

"You know what?" Abish suggested. "Give her back her things and we can ask her; whatever she says, that's how it will be."

"What's all these games for? Don't be a fool, Abish. You'd better tell your Avreml to back off from Rivele. That's the best he's going to get."

Bentshik got up from his chair. Avreml jumped to the door, turned its wide iron bolt, and stood there with arms crossed.

"We'll see about Rivele later," he said. "For now, I want the things."

Bentshik sat back in his seat and gave a look to Shaike Ox. Shaike understood. He got up and headed for the door.

Abish didn't move from his spot. He watched and waited to see what would happen. Freidl bit on her apron so she wouldn't scream. She took a quick glance at Abish. She saw that Abish's eyes were set on Shaike. She noticed his smile and settled down a little. She knew that as long as Abish was here, nothing terrible would happen to Avreml. She also knew she wasn't to get involved and she wasn't to make so much as a peep.

"Get away from the door!" Shaike ordered Avreml and raised his hand. But at the same instant, Avreml socked his face with a fist. It echoed through the house. Shaike fell to the ground doused in blood. Freidl screamed silently. Motke moved his chair to the corner of the room. Bentshik got up. Abish rose to counter him. It seemed like Abish had suddenly grown a head taller.

"Sit down!" Abish ordered Bentshik. He looked at Abish, whose giant size, flaming eyes, and wild beard shook him. He sat down. Freidl went into the kitchen, came right out with a bowl of water and a towel, and set to washing Shaike's bloodied face. Shaike groaned when he felt the cold water. His face had swelled. With one hand, Abish dragged the half-senseless Shaike away from the middle of the room and laid him out in the corner where Motke was sitting.

All of a sudden, Bentshik sprung up. A long knife flashed in his hand. Immediately he said, "Avreml, move away from the door."

Abish froze for a moment, but he quickly regained control of himself. He knew that Bentshik was deft with a knife, just like with his fists, and that the gang shuddered in fear of Bentshik's fists, but that his knife was even worse. With careful steps, Abish approached Bentshik, but Bentshik threw himself at Avreml and aimed his knife at Avreml's face. Avreml dodged it adroitly. Bentshik's knife cut deep into Avreml's arm. Avreml sprang into action. He pushed his father off to the side and kicked Bentshik in the stomach. Bentshik fell to the ground and the knife fell out of his hand. He got up fast and set his fists to fight with Avreml, but it was already too late. Avreml's fists hammered on Bentshik's head.

This all happened in one short minute. Catching his breath, Abish looked around at what had happened. With his experienced eyes he

"Get away from the door!" Shaike ordered Avreml and raised his hand.

appraised his son's strong, skilled work. He saw that his only son didn't need his help. He pressed Freidl to the wall with his shoulder and shielded her completely. He also guarded Shaike and Motke and watched Avreml and Bentshik keenly. Bentshik's legs started to wobble under the hail of clobbering. He fell to the ground. Avreml picked him up, leaned him against the wall, and kept on hammering. He didn't feel the pain of his gash and didn't notice the blood running from his arm. He didn't feel anything, didn't realize that his blows were breaking Bentshik's bones. Bentshik couldn't take it anymore and started to shriek, "What the hell! Save me! He's killing me!"

The neighbors ran over. They besieged the windows, which were veiled by curtains. They banged the door. Freidl struggled with all her strength to free herself from Abish, who was still holding her pressed against the wall. She started screaming, and her screams merged with Bentshik's cries for help. Motke sat shoved in the corner and shook. Shaike tried to get up but fell back to the floor.

Finally, Abish let Freidl go and tore Avreml off of Bentshik. Bentshik fell on the ground like a bale of hay. He sat up with a straining effort and propped himself up against the wall. Completely drenched in blood, he stopped screaming, starting to groan and cry instead.

Freidl fell on Avreml, but he pushed her away and went closer to Bentshik. Abish blocked the way with his large, heavy hand.

"That's enough son. You could still kill him."

In a loud voice, Avreml said, "I want Rivele's things. Or else I am gonna kill him. Where are Rivele's things?"

"I don't know," wailed Bentshik.

Avreml pushed his father away, picked Bentshik up from the ground, set him up against the wall, and started punching him again.

Motke was certain that Bentshik wouldn't get out alive from under Avreml's fists. He had seen bloody fights, and more than once watched slack jawed as Shaike Ox worked someone over. And he thought even higher of Bentshik's iron mitts. Just one clop from Bentshik could knock a guy unconscious. But Motke had never seen the kind of power and technique Avreml had shown in just a few minutes. He knew at once that even the entire gang couldn't compete with Abish and his son. He also knew that after what happened today, they wouldn't be able to hold their control over the gang, so he yelled, "Let him go Avreml, and I'll tell you where the stuff is." Avreml let go of Bentshik, who fell to the ground. Motke went to him and said, "Bentshik, tell them where the stuff is."

Bentshik was still crying.

People were starting to bang down the door. Berke Blizzard's voice tore through the shut door. Abish opened it. Berke, Khone, and Zeidl came into the house. Abish relocked the door. Berke asked in his alarming voice, "Is the thief here?" But when he saw what was going on in the house, he kept quiet.

"Tell them where the things are," Motke begged the obliterated Bentshik, even though he knew very well where the chests were hidden. But to go so far as to say himself where the things were, that he didn't dare.

Abish and Avreml stood next to Bentshik. Avreml felt a pain in his arm and noticed in that instant that his gash was bleeding. Freidl stood with Berke and his sons and cried quietly.

In speech broken up by sobbing, Bentshik said, "Who needs her things? I don't need them. It's all her fault. She played me for a fool. She accepted my gifts, a watch, a bracelet, a . . ."

Those last words hit Avreml like thunder. He realized that Rivele had never given him a clear answer when he asked where she had gotten those expensive pieces of jewelry. Meaning, Bentshik had given them to her, and she had accepted them from him.

"No way, it's a lie, couldn't be." Avreml tried to calm himself, but he knew it was not a lie, that Bentshik was telling the truth. And that ignited a wild hatred in him against Bentshik. Up until now, he had been Bentshik the Thief, and Avreml had beaten him up without rage, calculating that punches were the only way to return Rivele's trousseau to her. But now, he wasn't Bentshik the Thief anymore. He was Bentshik who had given gifts to Rivele, and from whom she had accepted them. He leaped against his rival and roared, "You thief, give up the things, or I'm gonna put an end to you here and now!"

He grabbed Bentshik, picked him up from the floor, and gave him a horrifying sock in the jaw. Bentshik let out a groan and dropped, knocked out cold.

Abish held his son back.

Motke ran up and said, "Reb Abish, tomorrow morning I'll bring the things to Rivele's house. I swear by my dead mother and father. Do you believe me Reb Abish?"

Abish grabbed his wide beard in his large hand, glanced at Motke, at Avreml, and then at Bentshik, and then at Motke again, and said calmly, "Motke, do you understand what you're saying? You're playing with the Angel of Death."

"You'll have the things tomorrow," said Motke. "I'll bring them myself."

Avreml didn't want to trust Motke, but he obeyed his father and agreed. Berke, Khone, and Zeidl helped Motke remove Shaike and Bentshik. Motke went in the middle, with Shaike and Bentshik at his sides, leaning on his shoulders. That's how they dragged themselves out of the house.

Motke kept his word. The next morning, a peasant brought all three chests on his wagon. Not one thing was missing. The gold jewelry that Rivele had received from Bentshik was packed, as before, in a small wooden box inside one of the chests.

8

Everyone in town seized on the news, and it spread like wildfire shaking up the town. Young and old talked breathlessly about the incident, telling and retelling it with all its details. Each narrator added a drop from their own imagination until the quiet and unassuming Avreml had suddenly risen to the status of a legendary hero in the town's eyes, possessing superhuman strength, ready to risk his life for justice.

For Abish the Bear, too, Avreml had suddenly grown up. As his father, he felt a warm and glowing joy, which both fortified and worried him. Although he loved his only child, Abish had often wondered how he had fathered such a son, so quiet and modest, in a way that wasn't quite fitting for a man. Avreml's refined bearing and appearance were the opposite of his father's, and it made Abish feel strangely distanced from his only son. His awareness of how different his son was from him had pained him, and although he kept it quiet, he resented his wife Freidl for giving him such a son. But, when he reminded himself of what he had gone through in his youth on account of his wild anger and strength, he consoled himself that Avreml was better off taking after his mother. "It's better this way," he used to think to himself as a reassurance.

But after that fight Avreml had with Shaike Ox and Bentshik, after he saw for himself his son's agility and strength, Abish felt that this was indeed his son, his own flesh and blood. He felt closer to Avreml, more related to him, and he loved him even more than before. But at the same time, Abish worried. He was afraid that Avreml would become someone else now that he had discovered his own strength. He remembered how he himself, when he was young, had immediately felt like a new person, a different Abish, after his first fight. But his pride in Avreml's newly displayed strength wasn't diminished by his worry that his son might follow in his footsteps down a crooked path. His house felt even more like home. Freidl had become even more dear to him, and he truly felt that Avreml was his own child, a limb of his own body. He was glad to have another man in the house, another Abish the Bear, albeit a younger and better looking one. He felt like he was starting a new life, a life with purpose.

Neither Abish nor Freidl suspected that Avreml was so tormented by jealousy. They figured he wasn't going to work because of the gash on his arm he had taken from Bentshik the Thief. They were pleased he was staying at home until the wound healed.

Actually, the wound didn't bother Avreml much at all. He barely felt the physical pain, due to the other, internal pain, which tortured him with no respite. With agonizing clarity, he replayed his memories of conversations with Rivele about the expensive jewelry she was so excited about. He had asked her a few times where she had gotten such expensive things, and each time she dodged his questions with strange answers, saying she hadn't stolen them, that she'd gotten them for free. Now he didn't need to ask anymore. Now he knew that Bentshik had given her those gifts, and that she had accepted them from him. Why had Bentshik given her gifts? And why had she accepted them? What kind of business was she in with Bentshik the Thief?

Questions like those kept pounding in his head and burning like fire. That pain was a lot stronger than the pain from the knife wound Bentshik had given him. No matter how much he tried to convince himself that it was nothing, that it was foolishness, he couldn't ease his heartache. The more he tried to console himself, the further he sank into his dismal thoughts. He let them wander unhampered, letting his imagination torment him, painting pictures of Bentshik and Rivele's love affair for him. Those images, which he created himself, became the solid truth for him. He had become incapable of distinguishing what was true and what was made up. He was certain that Rivele had played him for a fool and carried on a romance with Bentshik, who was completely innocent, because Rivele had, it turns out, played her cat-and-mouse game with him too, and Bentshik had only started the whole scandal because of her phony tricks! He couldn't forgive her trickery and how it had dragged him into a conflict with Bentshik and his gang.

One thing was clear to him: it was over between him and Rivele! He would never marry such a phony girl. He would always be doubting her about one thing or another. And if she acted this falsely before the wedding, surely she would behave even worse after. But what should he do? How would he get out of the engagement? Should he go to her and say everything to her face or write her a letter? Or should he send for Rivele's brothers, his friends Khone and Zeidl, and tell them the whole story? What would they say? How would people look at him? He knew the town jumped on this kind of thing. It wouldn't be a secret to anyone why he had canceled the engagement. People would talk badly about him, pity him, and make fun of him. And what's more, he felt bad for his good, quiet mother. She had endured so much because of his father, and now she would suffer from her son, too. His anger at Rivele for bringing all this misfortune on everyone raged ever more wildly within him.

Avreml decided he had to get away from the town, and maybe even take his mother and father with him. But where to? To America! The thought came to him like lightning. Yes, America! That answered everything. He could start over from scratch there. In America he wouldn't be Avreml, Abish the Bear's son. There, he'd be called Avrohom Broide. He could go first, and then he'd send for his parents. He'd come back to town to get them. Why not? He was young and strong, he could work day and night, save up enough money, and then come to town as a rich, dressed-up American, and take his mother and father off to America. If his parents tried to stop him, he'd go without their permission, or even without them knowing. Yes, America is his only rescue, the only remedy to all his problems. He will go off to America and be through with Bentshik, through with Rivele, through with the whole town! America! That's what he'd do. No one could hold him back. And he shouldn't delay. If he's going, he's going soon—tomorrow, the day after tomorrow, the sooner the better. Tomorrow he'll take his money out of the bank, the money he had been saving for his wedding with Rivele, for furniture, and for his own workshop. He can leave a portion for his father, and the rest will cover a ship ticket.

SECOND PART

THE CITY OF NEW YORK

1

America didn't go as well for Avreml as he had imagined. The assimilation process was hard for him, and it was difficult to feel at home in the big city of New York. The large tombstone-like buildings threw him into a panic. His dark little room, with its itty-bitty window blocked by a brick wall, enclosed him in loneliness like a prison cell and drove him out to the street. Out there, the wild commotion and the strangeness of the streets drove him back into the dark little room.

He had a hard time uttering the few English words that he had toiled for weeks to learn. He began to lose hope of ever learning the difficult, weird language.

He also didn't have any luck finding a job. He worked at *pey-per bok-ses*, at *po-ket-boox*, and at a dozen other jobs before he finally succeeded in learning *a treyd*. A guy from the old country brought him into a *shap* where they taught him to become a *for-ree-er* and make coats from pelts. He had to work four weeks for free and pay ten dollars on top of that. He felt satisfied though, knowing he would finally have a trade under his belt and could start making a living.

Avreml hated the shop. He hated the discipline of the shop. He couldn't stand how the workers feared the *bos*, who ran around like a wildman among the workers all day grumbling, "Get a move on, the day's not standing still!" He couldn't understand why the workers shuddered to speak a word to each other, why they had such a fear of the boss, that skinny pale little guy who never got tired of running around the shop, eyeing the work and watching each laborer's movement. It was crowded in the shop, with the tables and machines arranged so close to each other—on purpose, so the boss could have each of them under his eye. The floor was cluttered with heaps of pelts and partially sewn coats. Wet coats lay by the nail boards, having been soaked to become softer for nailing. Next to the tables, at which the *kat-ters* stood to cut, and next to the machines on which the *op-per-rey-ters* sewed, lay little pieces of cut-off fur mixed up with staples, which the cutters had used to pin one pelt to another. Piles of fabric scraps, trimmed from the linings, lay next to

the *fee-nee-shers'* tables. Little nails that the nailer had used were scattered
all over the floor. The entire dirty shop had a coating of hair dust from
the fur. The windows were always dirty. In the hot summer days, the shop
was unbearable. Hot air and dust bit at your nose and poked your throat.
Sweat streamed like water. The fur's cheap dye colored the workers' moist
hands and got smeared across their faces. Avreml grew to fear looking
at the workers. What made the worst impression on him was when the
workers consoled him by saying, "Don't worry greenhorn, you'll get used
to this misery."

In the evenings after work, Avreml would go out on his building's
ruf to cool off from the heat and to breathe in a little fresh air. The nights
were even harder than the days. Freed from work, he gave himself over
to his longing for the shtetl. His homesickness tortured him to tears. He
missed the wide green fields where he strolled on cool summer nights,
the smooth spacious river where he used to swim worry free on summer
nights and on Shabbos. He missed the cool, fresh water and pouring
it into the heavy wooden bucket. He missed his father and mother, his
friends, and he was just dying from yearning for Rivele, whom he loved
now more than ever. The nights were simply painful for him. His tired
limbs pulled him toward sleep, but his longing for home and his regrets
about losing his mind and coming to America wouldn't let him fall asleep.
He isolated himself from everyone and didn't make any friends. He was
all alone in the big city of New York, lost in his loneliness and seclusion.
He gave himself over to his yearning and his regret with a painful pleasure. Stubbornly, he avoided the amusements of the big city and the big
country so he could rescue himself from them and return home as soon
as possible.

At first, he thought of going to Brazil or to Argentina, but he realized
those were empty thoughts, and he was just fooling himself. In truth, he
really wanted to go home, to the shtetl where he was born, where he grew
up, where everyone knew him and he knew everyone, where life flowed
restfully and without worry, among his own people and friends. But how
could he go home? How would people look at him in the shtetl, and
would Rivele forgive him for hurting her like he had and then leaving
without saying goodbye? He thought about it and thought about it, and

"Get a move on, the day's not standing still!"

couldn't find any answer. He frightened himself with the thought that he would have to stay in America. He often asked himself disapprovingly what made him so different from his acquaintances. They were all so satisfied with America and wouldn't go back home for anything. He was the only one who tortured himself and couldn't adapt to the new life. He tried to force himself to adjust to the strange land with such thinking, but the shop, the gloomy room, and the loneliness drove him back to his homesickness.

Avreml's nerves were getting more and more rattled. He began worrying about his health. He knew that no doctor would be able to help him. "Ach," he said to himself, "if only I had a friend, someone I could speak to from the heart, then it would probably be easier." But where do you find a close friend like that, someone you can talk to freely and frequently, someone who will understand?

Morris, thought Avreml, *is the only one I could complain to. Smart and experienced, Morris would definitely understand.* But he didn't know how to approach the topic. Morris worked with him in the shop. He was a cutter. A tall, big-boned, middle-aged man, always neatly dressed, with a kind, masculine face and friendly black eyes. Morris gave the impression of a worldly person with a lot of life experience. All the workers in the shop treated Morris with respect. Even the boss, Morris's uncle, treated him differently than the other workers. The boss never dared tell him to "get a move on." To Morris he spoke with dignity, like he would to one of the *bay-yers* who purchase for large companies, or to the president of a bank. He consulted with him about the business. If a fight broke out between two workers in the shop, Morris could smooth out the conflict because the workers gladly deferred to his reason and fairness.

From the first time Avreml saw Morris, he took a liking to him. Whenever he would ask, "Nu, Avreml, how's it going in America?" Avreml could hear a special friendliness in his voice.

He made up his mind that he would wait for Morris at the shop after work, spill his heart out to him, and ask for some advice. But he put it off day after day because he couldn't work up the courage to have that kind of a conversation with Morris. Even so, just the decision to talk it through with Morris calmed him a bit. Once, when his homesickness had set in on torturing him again, Morris's image started swimming in front of his eyes, like a loyal ally in a hostile land. Finally, he decided that tomorrow he would tell Morris he wanted to talk to him after work.

That day, Avreml got up earlier than usual. He got dressed quickly and went out to the street. It was still early, but the sun was already burning the stone city, which hadn't even cooled off from the night's heat. All over the streets, people were walking to work with slow, sleepy strides. In their damp faces, Avreml saw their exhaustion from the suffocating sleepless night.

He went into the little restaurant across from the shop, took two rolls, a butter pat, and a cup of coffee, then took a seat by a little table away from the other people sitting at their little tables and sluggishly eating their meals.

Morris came into the restaurant with his typical firm and confident steps. He took a cup of coffee and nodded to the people who were sitting at the little tables with a long glance. He noticed Avreml, sitting alone at the little table and approached him.

"May I sit next to you Avreml?" he asked in a cheerful friendly voice.

"Certainly," answered Avreml, pleased and blushing.

Morris hadn't waited for his answer. He pulled out a chair that had been pushed under the table, made himself comfortable, and began slowly sipping his coffee. Abruptly, he let out a quick question, "So, Avreml, have you made your peace with 'Columbus's Country'[1] yet?"

The directness of the question shook Avreml. He was pleased that Morris had sat down beside him. It gave him a thrill that he was speaking so formally to him. It showed he respected him. Morris didn't wait for Avreml's answer, and continued talking between one sip of coffee and the next. "You're not the first guy to have a hard time adjusting to life in America. It was rough for me, too, my first couple of years. I was homesick. I didn't want to stay here for nothing. I thought this was a wild place."

Avreml slurped up Morris's words.

---

1   A colloquial term for the United States.

"But now," continued Morris, "I wouldn't go back for nothing, not even if my entire hometown sent for me. That's just how it goes Avreml."

He pushed aside the emptied coffee cup, turned his face to Avreml, looked him right in the eye, and said pointedly, "Avreml, America is the finest country in the world. My uncle's dirty shop isn't America. Working at my uncle's shop, which is truly a torture, is not America. Here in the New World, life flows with a mighty force. Everything that goes on here is in order to make the worker's life easier and better. You Avreml, you've got to adjust to this life. You've got to forget your hometown, and you've got to find your way into this beautiful and fruitful American life. It will get better."

Avreml couldn't get over his surprise. How did Morris know his thoughts about what a hard time he was having, even his homesickness, and his opinions about America? With a stammer, he asked, "So, how does a person find his way?"

Morris was silent for a while, smoking a cigarette as he gazed into Avreml's face, and in a confident, even commanding tone told him, "Sign up to the union! Tomorrow night after work there's going to be a mass meeting at Cooper Union Hall.[2] Come to the meeting."

He offered Avreml a pamphlet calling all furriers to the meeting.

"Nu, it's getting late, let's get back to our slave labor," he said, ending the conversation. They left the restaurant and went up to the shop.

Avreml knew the trade had a union. From listening to the talk among the workers, he had gathered that after losing the strike in 1920, the union had become so weak that it had completely lost control of the shops. He also knew that his shop was one of the many that didn't belong to the union, and that his boss was one of the union's stingiest opponents.

Avreml didn't have anything against the union. In fact, he had even considered becoming a member. But for the life of him, he couldn't understand how the union would help him with his personal problems. At the

---

2   A nine-hundred-person auditorium at Cooper Union College in New York's Lower East Side. Many labor unions, including the Furriers Union, and notable progressive speakers used the hall for mass meetings.

same time, he was sure that Morris was smart and wouldn't give him any useless advice.

Avreml waited impatiently for the mass meeting. He was one of the first to arrive at the enormous Cooper Union Hall and chose a seat close to the platform. Little by little, the hall filled with workers. The place started to buzz. The workers were all speaking to one another in loud voices. Avreml sat by himself and observed the others. He hadn't known there were so many furriers. He found it strange how different they looked compared to the workers in his shop. They were all clean shaven and neatly dressed. They laughed and joked with their friends and neighbors. Even sitting still and silent, he felt like one of them, and he started to feel love for this lively and sociable mass of workers.

A few people appeared on the platform. Loud applause broke out in the hall. When the chairman banged his gavel on the podium, the buzz cut off, as if by a knife. A resolute sincerity took over the faces of all the assembled workers. The chairman, a person in his fifties, seemed calm and relaxed. He explained that ever since the failed strike, the union had grown weaker, and the number of non-union shops had increased so that those thousands of workers weren't paying *dyuz* to the union. He explained that the bosses knew what state the union was in. They knew that the union didn't have enough power to protect the worker, and they used the situation to their advantage, reducing wages and extending working hours. There was a danger that the old slave wages, which used to rule the trade before the union was founded, would be reinstated in the shops. He also announced that the travesty of home work was starting to get reintroduced in the trade. He ended with a rousing call for the workers to join the union once again and refortify the organization so they could bring back union wages, union conditions, and union control to the trade. The workers ardently applauded the chairman.

After that, he introduced a union official as the next speaker. This one spoke in English. Avreml didn't understand all of it, but he was fairly certain that he was saying almost the same things as the chairman had before in Yiddish. When the speaker was finished with his speech, the chairman banged his gavel and asked everyone to come to order because the next speaker was the great worker-leader who had helped build all the needle-trade unions, "The dedicated friend of the Furriers' Union, the great leader of the Socialist Party, beloved to us all, Mr. M."[3]

A thunder of applause broke out in the hall. The speaker approached the podium. Avreml took a good look at him. He was just a bit too tall to be called short, and was thin and straight as an arrow. He had a noble face and wore gold-rimmed eyeglasses on his narrow, pointed nose. The speaker removed his eyeglasses, set them inside a leather case, and put the case into the upper pocket of his jacket. While the speaker was calmly dealing with his eyeglasses, he spoke softly, richly, with a pleasant, unpolished voice. He said that when he comes to speak to the furriers, they clobber him, but he feels at home. The audience laughed. But when he goes to speak to the bosses, he said, they don't clobber him, yet he feels beat up. "What good is your applause though?" he said. "Better you should build a robust union and I will applaud you—and the bosses will stop beating us all up."

"In election times," he complained, "it's more of the same. I speak before large enthusiastic crowds and receive hearty applause, but my opponent, the bosses' representative, receives the votes when *el-ek-shen* day comes. Now he sits in Congress, and I, your true representative, sit at home."

Again, the audience gave an affable laugh. Avreml didn't understand why they were laughing. To him, this sounded like a serious and sorrowful matter that wasn't appropriate to laugh at.

Abruptly, the speaker let out a bellow:

"You laugh? This is not a joke! It is time for the worker to wake up to the sad truth already!"

His calmness vanished. He was shooting his words into the crowd like hot bullets from a gun. Avreml got swept up in the speaker's passionate, insightful, and forceful speech. He observed how his thin, noble face burned red with fire. His voice rose higher and higher and thundered with power. Avreml sat hypnotized. The speaker's words streamed right

---

3   Meyer London, Socialist Party congressman representing the Lower East Side of Manhattan in the US House of Representatives in 1915–1919 and 1921–1923.

into his heart and his mind. He could have sat and listened to him all night long.

Then, unexpectedly, the speaker began speaking in a softer, more lyrical voice. He spoke of how the time was not far off when the working class would be organized and would seize the entire government apparatus in its own hands, abolishing slavery and exploitation. It would end bloody wars and lead us to a world of justice, fairness, brotherhood, culture, peace, and progress, to the world of socialism.

When the speaker finished, the hall thundered with applause. Avreml woke, as if from a deep sleep, and clapped his hands with all his might. His clapping rang out over the entire hall.

When he stepped out of the hall, he sensed a great energy filling his limbs. He knew that something had happened to him, but he couldn't tell just what it was. He walked through the streets with such ease and vitality he felt as if he were floating on air. The big city streets and the tall buildings, which had always seemed like gravestones to him, and the bustle of the street, which he had found so odious, suddenly became genial and cozy. Everyone he saw seemed like a dear old friend.

Now Avreml understood Morris's wisdom in advising him to attend the meeting and join the union. He recalled Morris's words: "You've got to find your way into American life."

He started talking to himself, not noticing that the people walking by were staring and smirking at him. "Thank you Morris, my friend. Thank you for showing me the way." Now for the first time, he could fully understand what Morris had meant when he said his uncle's dirty shop is not America. He thought: how different the workers looked at the assembly! Nothing like in the shop. There in the shop, fear of the boss dominated. Everyone hurried to get as much work done as they could, and each person's face was smeared with subjugation. It was every man for himself there, and every one of them was a part of the machine. But at the meeting, it was an entirely different scene. There, each person was a part of the broad, brotherly, genial mass, throbbing with excitement and strength. Speech, feeling, excitement—the workers had understood the speaker so well! Avreml had also understood each word, even though he had never heard a speech like that before.

Avreml had experienced everything the speaker said as so clear, so elemental. It was only natural that the workers should absorb his words in a still tension and applaud him so fervently. How would it even be possible not to be in agreement with such a speech and with such people? He recalled how he himself had suddenly stopped feeling like a stranger among the workers, and how his loneliness completely disappeared, and he had become his own person, just like the people sitting around him. He felt embraced by a queer warmth and a closeness toward all of them. He had an urge to scream out his joy, but together with the others, he squeezed out the joy into hand clapping, and the clapping lifted him even higher, making it seem even more like a holiday.

So this is America! he thought. *This is what Morris was talking about: workers' meetings, unions, freedom, equality, brotherhood, socialism. It's wonderful!* His muscles tightened with a swelling energy. He could sense his blood flowing hotly through his veins. It seemed like he was truly seeing the world in its full light. Everything looked brand new to him, as if he were seeing it for the very first time. He understood now that America wasn't at all what he had thought. Now he freshly understood that America was, as the speaker had said, not only a new land but also a continuation of a great beginning, and that it would lead to tremendous developments. And everything depended on the workers!

Avreml's resentment of America vanished. So did his homesickness for his little hometown. He could tell that in this new America he had become a new man, completely unlike the Avreml of yesterday.

Tomorrow, yes, tomorrow morning, he thought, *I'm going to go up to Morris in the shop and tell him softly, but firmly, "Mister Morris, I've made my peace with Columbus's Country. I've found the way!"*

2

Avreml became a union member. He threw his heart and soul into union activity. His own problems lost their earlier sting and became unimportant. His personal life became intertwined with the life of the masses. He no longer missed home and didn't even think about the old country. His entire youth seemed an incidental, foreign phase of his life. If he thought about what had happened to him back home, it only amused him.

He wasn't dreaming about the past now but of the future, the beautiful and liberated life in which all of humanity would flourish. In the unions, he could see the pillars of the new world that were already forming, even if others hadn't noticed.

It was only the internal struggle within the union, between the left-wing opposition and the right-wing leadership,[1] that dimmed and wilted his hopeful spirits. He couldn't stand the harsh criticisms the left wing wielded against the right-wing union leadership, whom he deeply respected as the workers' representatives. He found it painful that the struggle divided the workers into two camps, damaging them all. It also upset him when the conflicts spread out into the open, dragging down the union's reputation. Out of these frustrations, he became a firm opponent to the left-wingers and spoke out against them at every opportunity. This led the right-wing union leadership to bring him nearer to them. With their help, he got elected to the *eg-zek-yu-teev* (the managing committee) of his *lo-kul*, which made him truly happy. Now, he thought, he'd have a real opportunity to help realize the workers' holy dream of building the beautiful new free world. He promised himself that his first major task would be to unite the left wing with the right wing in the union and bring their conflicts to an end. The battles were growing more caustic every day and were putting the whole union in grave danger.

His hopes, however, were not realized. The deeper he became entrenched

---

1   The left wing and right wing of the Furriers Union, like much of the labor movement and the political left, played out as a conflict between the Communist and Socialist parties, respectively.

in the right camp, the more all sorts of doubts about their leadership and plans started disturbing him. Before, when he was on the outside and could only observe from a distance, it seemed like everything the leaders did was smooth and decent. But when he entered the inner circle he saw them as just the opposite.

He couldn't understand why the union leadership didn't love the workers. It was deeply disappointing to him how some of the leaders openly showed their disdain for the workers. He couldn't stand the union leaders' indifference to the workers' hardships. Their cynicism vexed him and drove him to bitterness.

Little by little, Avreml came to understand that crooks dominated the union; that a lot of the shops were protected by genuine crooks, gangsters even; and that the union leaders themselves didn't dare set foot in the "protected" shops, even though the working conditions were very bad there. He admitted to himself that some of the union leaders were simply not honorable men. He learned that the *o-fis* was run by a system of corruption. He discovered that union leaders had "safeguarded" enough money from the strike fund to "go into business" right after the strike. It became clear to him that the union leadership was absolutely not invested in the workers—not in their struggles, and not in their ideals.

These were things Avreml half knew and half suspected until that terrible night that hit him like a thunderclap and set off a real crisis in his life.

Everyone in the office was seriously agitated about the conflicts among the *bo-yes*, meaning the young guys. That's what people called the thugs and bandits from the two gangs that both worked for the right wing. There was a rivalry flaring up between the two gangs, and it was leading to open fighting. The workers talked about it with scorn and derision.

"It will iron itself out," said some furriers. "They're their own problem."

Others stood up for the gangsters with a bitter laugh. "The boyes are right. The leadership is propping themselves up with the gangs' strength, so let them blow through some money. Why should the gang in the office get everything and the other gangs nothing? You wanna have loyal boyes, you gotta pay up."

The situation became serious. The battles between the boyes became an open scandal. There were bloody fistfights in the street, in broad day-light, and hundreds of workers hanging around the fur market[2] witnessed brawls between the gangsters. Once even, one gangster shot another one, right on the spot. The news traveled quickly through the shops and wor-ried the workers sick.

"They should just have a big shoot-out so we can be rid of them," people said in the shops. "They've spilled enough workers' blood. Now that they're murdering each other, maybe they'll give the workers a rest."

The top union leaders were shocked, as were leaders of other unions in the right camp, who also used boyes to prop up their leadership. Tele-phones were phoned and conferences held.

Finally, the *tsheef* of the Strong Guards, a figure fat as a barrel with a big bloated face, called for a meeting to patch up the split. Avreml was one of the executive members who was asked to attend the meeting as well. The chief opened the meeting with a speech.

He said, "Boyes, this can't go on any longer. It's going to end with all of us packed in prison and the lefties and Communist *bes-terdz* taking over the union. I invited all the boyes from both gangs, and even a few executive members, so that you can straighten this out once and for all. *Doun-toun* sent word that we've got to straighten this out. You get me? That's all I've got to say. Now you can talk. But with your mouths, boyes, not with your fists."

Several brawny young men started speaking at once.

The chief, from his seat on the platform, banged his gavel on the table and screamed, "*Siddoun!* We're gonna talk one at a time, like at a regular union meeting. *Sit doun!*" When everyone had gone back to their places, the chief said with satisfaction, "Oh key, boyes. Now, who wants the floor?"

Two young guys, who were sitting in separate rows among their own boyes, Bulletproof Chickie, a short, big-boned popular fellow with little green eyes, and Semke the Baby, a big-shouldered giant with two pole-like arms, both yelled at once that they wanted the floor and stood up. They looked at each other with dagger eyes.

---

2   The area in Manhattan from Twenty-Sixth to Thirtieth Streets, between Sixth and Eighth Avenues, where fur shops are concentrated.

The chief was at a loss. He looked first at Bulletproof Chickie, and then at Semke the Baby, and back at Chickie, and couldn't figure out who should speak first.

"Hey Alex," yelled some of the boyes. "No *po-li-tiks*! Let the Baby speak!"

"Nothing doing!" yelled others. "Bulletproof is gonna speak first."

"*Shad-dap!*" bellowed dozens of voices at once, setting off a new uproar. Half of the room got up on their feet ready to fight.

The chief banged his gavel yelling, "Sit down! Order! Quiet boyes! No fights!"

When it had quieted down, the chief wiped off his fat inflated face, which had become red and sweaty, and said, "The leftist bastards act better at their meetings than we do."

"Hey, don't go preaching morals to us!" yelled one of the boyes. "Focus on deciding who should speak first and STOP LECTURING!"

"*Dat's rayt!*" said others in approval.

The chief was silent for a moment. Finally, he issued his ruling. "I'm flipping a coin: heads Bulletproof talks first, tails the Baby."

Applause broke out.

Avreml was sitting in a corner, not believing his own eyes and ears. He had never seen or heard anything like this.

The chief tossed a half-dollar in the air. The room got quiet. All eyes watched the coin's flight.

When the half-dollar lay on the table, Bulletproof Chickie and Semke the Baby ran up to it. Their heads, together with the chief's head, bent over it.

"Tails!" shouted the chief. The Baby had the floor.

The boyes sitting on the right side of the room clapped. The others bucked, howled, and yowled like cats. Several of the boyes treated the chief to some vulgar noises.

The chief banged his gavel.

When the room quieted down, Semke the Baby started his speech:

"Now lissen, wise guys, I'm gonna say what I want, even if you scream your guts out! No one *bool-doze-ez* me!"

"What makes you think you're such a big shot?" yelled Bulletproof.

A fresh uproar broke out. "Sit down!" "Shut up!" "Kick 'im out!" "You louse!" and other various shouts filled up the crowded hall.

The chief banged his gavel. The sweat was running down his puffy red face.

Finally it quieted down. The chief said, "Boyes, we've got to get this straightened out tonight. These stunts don't help any. Downtown has told us to straighten this out. You know Downtown don't fall for no bluff. If we don't straighten this out ourselves tonight, Downtown is going to come up to the office and *kleen* us out. *Dat's oll!*"

"Where'd you hear that?" asked Bulletproof.

"Where'd I hear that?" repeated the chief mechanically before answering brief and sharp. "Big Gengi himself was in the office. He told me so. Tough Sholem heard. Right Tough?" The chief turned to one of the boyes.

Tough Sholem answered, "Dat's rayt, Alex."

The chief kept talking. "Big Gengi told me the boss won't tolerate any *roff stoff* between the boyes in the Furriers Union. Now do you finally get it? Downtown means *bizness!*"

The hall got quiet. The meeting had been brought under control, as if by magic.

Semke the Baby said, "We're going to straighten it out, but we want a *skver deel*. No *fei-vo-rits*. We do the *doirty* work, just the same as Chickie's gang. We shut down shops that don't pay *dyuz*. We beat up the leftist bastards at the meetings. We want *fifti-fifti*."

"We're no *dommies*," the Baby said to the chief. "Almost all the contractors pay. Hundreds of shops are under control. They get *pro-tek-shun* and they pay. Regular *in-nish-ee-yaish-en* fees from the *kan-di-dates* who want to join the union come in every week.[3] So where's the dough disappearing to? Some union leaders are taking a cut, and that's on top of what they themselves are already getting from the bosses, which is already enough. When a boy gets in trouble or sprung from the *kool-er*, and he needs help, we don't turn him away. We all put in our fair share. So, when it comes to this divvying up here, we're going to do that even Steven, too.

---

3   The Union required workers at unionized shops to pay regular dues as well as initiation fees. When they used gangsters to collect the fees, the gangs took a cut.

And we will also keep track," shouted the Baby, "of how much *rev-in-yu* comes in. A square deal. No *mon-ki biz-ness*! You get me?"

Bulletproof Chickie jumped up as if a snake had bitten him. His face was fire red. His green eyes burned like a tiger's. He yelled, "If you don't like it Baby, you can go back to the pimp racket where you came from."

"You *skweel-er!*" howled the Baby and went after Chickie with both fists.

A wild fight exploded. Everyone got tangled up into one ball of bodies. A few boyes lay on the floor. The Baby stood in the center of the body ball, clobbering at heads, faces, and spines with both his fists.

"Cops! The cops are coming!" yelled the chief.

At that instant the fighting stopped. Most of the boyes went back to their seats like well-trained soldiers and fixed up their hair and ties with nervous fingers. A few boyes sat turned aside in the edges of the room wiping blood from their noses with handkerchiefs. A strained stillness had taken over the modest hall.

The chief exited the hall. A few minutes later he came back and resumed his honorary place.

"Well, boyes, it looks like Downtown is going to have to straighten this out. You're all acting like a bunch of dumb kids, not like *Or-gin-niz-ey-shen boyes.*"

"Let Downtown straighten it out. In any case, I'm going to settle things with Chickie outside," said the Baby belligerently.

"I've filled guys bigger than you with lead," Bulletproof Chickie calmly answered Semke.

"Oh yeah?" asked Semke the Baby with hostile sarcasm.

"Step outside, you worthless lug. I'll show you" replied Chickie with anger.

"Let's go! You think you're such a tough guy!" Semke the Baby challenged Chickie. He got up, folded his arms across his chest, and called again, "Alright, come on, you worm!"

Chickie rose from his seat resolutely. His mouth twisted to one side. His green eyes shot a bitter look.

The boyes were paralyzed with fright. Avreml shuddered. He couldn't believe he was awake. It all seemed like a bad dream.

"Chickie!" hollered the chief. Chickie turned his head to the chief. Everyone's eyes fixed on the chief.

Two revolvers glinted from both of the chief's hands. He got down from the platform and took a few short, measured steps, not shifting his eyes from Chickie.

"Stick 'em up Chickie! I mean business," said the chief with a professional calm.

Chickie obeyed and raised his hands. He knew from experience that when the chief pulled out his guns, he used them.

"Sit down, Baby, and shut up!" commanded the chief in the same calm, matter-of-fact tone. Semke the Baby sat down.

"Sholem!" called the chief.

"Yes, Alex," answered Tough Sholem obediently.

"Empty out Chickie's pockets."

Tough Sholem, the chief's right-hand man, went up to Chickie, turned out his pockets, and pulled out a revolver from his breast pocket. He put the revolver in one of his own pants pockets, and coolly returned to his spot.

"Chickie," the chief said in a hard voice. "I warned you to come to this meeting without a rod. Why didn't you do like I told you? Are you an organization boy, or do you take the law into your own hands?"

Chickie wanted to answer, but the chief, who was standing firmly next to him, gave him a hard sock in the stomach. Chickie fell to the chair under him.

No one dared make a move.

"And now, listen up you lousy schoolkids!" said the chief, holding both revolvers in his hands. "You're going to take orders from Downtown, or you can order up your gravestones for the cemetery. *On-der-stend?* You're all coming to the office tomorrow, just like nothing happened. Do you understand what I'm telling you? Big Gengi himself is going to straighten out all of the arguments. OK?"

"OK!" cried out everyone with satisfaction.

The chief ordered anyone who was coming into the office tomorrow to give the sign. Each man, without exception, raised his hand.

"And now," the chief directed, "Chickie and Sammy, *sheyk hends*! Like *reg-yu-la* boyes!"

"OK boyes, who wants the floor?" asked the chairman.

They both complied. The other boyes applauded and laughed.

The chief put the revolvers in his back pants pockets, took out his handkerchief, and wiped the sweat from his puffy face.

"Now boyes, let's all go to Uncle's and live it up a bit. But remember, keep your mouths shut."

The boyes shook the chief's hands.

"You did a fine job, Chief," they praised him. The chief smiled in satisfaction.

Avreml did not go with the boyes to live it up. He went home. He was bewildered and in pain. He couldn't get over his astonishment, his disgust. He was burning up. He felt like he had just been betrayed, robbed, and spit on: his insides were all emptied out.

"Chickie. The Baby. Tough Sholem," he said to himself. "Phooey! How horrible! It's just not possible! They're actually underworld gangsters! How did they get involved in a workers union? For crying out loud, what is going on here? And what about me? What should I do?" Avreml was on fire.

It seemed to him like he wouldn't be able to endure it.

3

Avreml started to feel constrained in the union. In place of his former respect, contempt for the union leadership now soaked through him. He stepped back from his union activities and cut off all contact with his union friends.

But he couldn't live without the labor movement. Without union activities, his life became hollow and pointless. He couldn't find any other interests in life. Still, going back into the union was impossible. The image of the meeting with the boyes was always in his head. He also couldn't stay silent about the rotten state of the union. But he didn't know what to do in order to save the union.

He decided to talk it through with his old friend Morris. He was sure that Morris's smarts would help him again and show him the right way.

Morris had become a manufacturer. Since he had first "gone into business," Avreml hadn't seen him often, even though he knew Morris was an important member of the Socialist Party. He decided to pay him a visit.

Morris received Avreml like an old friend. He showed him around his shop, bragged that he ran a kosher union shop, and led his guest into his private office where he carried on a long conversation.

"Avreml," said Morris, "I am a boss, but I still believe in socialism. I'm still a member of the Socialist Party. Socialism is a beautiful dream that will be realized in a hundred years' time, or two hundred years. Practical people can't wait for socialism."

Morris noticed Avreml's twisted expression and continued speaking. "I was active in the movement through all of my younger years. I did my part. I slaved for someone else long enough. Now others are making a profit for me. I am a successful businessman. I make money. I live comfortably. But I am also a good Socialist. One doesn't exclude the other. All practical Socialists are also successful businessmen."

Avreml didn't say anything. He wanted to end the conversation as quickly as possible. But Morris wouldn't stop preaching. "When you get older, Avreml, you'll get tired too. You'll get practical and go into business as well. You'll live comfortably, and I hope you'll stay true to your Socialist ideals, just like all of us older Socialists."

"Nu, Morris, we'll see about that later," answered Avreml with a marked impatience. "Right now I'm thinking about something else, and not about business."

He said goodbye to Morris quickly and left. Obviously, after a sermon like that he couldn't tell Morris the reason he had come. Morris's philosophy disgusted and shocked him. *Is that really the tragic end for all Socialists?* he thought.

Now he was beginning to understand why the union leaders had more respect for the bosses than for the workers, why they were more friendly with the bosses than with the union members. It had become clear to him that all of the union leaders he knew were actually future businessmen, only temporarily union leaders. That's why their orientation to the workers, to the unions, and to the workers' problems, was so indifferent and cynical. It's why they thought of every earnest, idealistic union member as a naive dreamer. *With that kind of attitude to the union and to the workers,* he thought, *it's no surprise at all that the union leadership developed such a corrupt system.*

He also started to understand why the struggle between the left wing and the right wing was so fierce and so frequently embittered. He recalled how the left-wingers spoke passionately against the union leadership, and he said to himself: "Of course, they're right. And how!"

After that visit with Morris, Avreml started befriending the left-wingers and talking with them like comrades, without any prejudice. When the left-wingers invited him to a meeting of their group, he accepted.

Avreml came back to life at that meeting of the left-wing group. The left-wingers were speaking in his language. They expressed clearly and fiercely the same thoughts that had been troubling him. He felt embraced by the warm camaraderie in the air. He appreciated their enthusiasm, and their deep faith in the masses, in the leaders of the Trade Union Educational League,[1] and in the Communist Party. He was entirely in agreement with their program.

---

1   The Trade Union Educational League (TUEL) was established by William Z. Foster in 1920 to "bore from within" AFL unions and advance radicalism and industrial organizing.

Avreml became a left-winger. Again, he threw himself into union activities, but this time he felt a solid ground under his feet. Life became interesting again. Once more he felt that his personal problems dissolved into the problems of the community, of his class. The way was marked out, and the goal was clear.

With heart and soul, he threw himself into the left's struggle against the corrupt leadership of his union and other unions. Each success inspired and motivated him to the next struggle. He had found what he had been searching for. He had discovered a new, flourishing world, his world.

4

As soon as the Furriers Union elected a left-wing administration,[1] all the right-wing officials from all the other needle-trade unions laid in on them. Using their widely read daily Yiddish newspaper[2] as a mouthpiece, they launched a slew of attacks and libels against the furriers' new leadership. The right wing and their newspaper presented themselves as Socialists and friends of the workers, but Avreml could finally see they weren't motivated at all by the workers' needs. Their own egotistical interest was the only force that drove them. The way the right wing hurled their shameless attacks against the union's new leadership convinced Avreml even further that they were truly in league with the bosses, and the bosses, of course, were completely intent on breaking the union.

When the union called a general strike, all of Avreml's suspicions were confirmed. He saw how the bosses, the gangsters, the police, and the right-wing so-called Socialist leaders worked hand in hand to break the strike.

Avreml put his all into the strike. He became an influential member of the General Strike Committee, where a substantial group considered him their leader. Even those who didn't still held him in high esteem. He was well loved among the masses of strikers and took on the Strike Committee's most challenging tasks. He had no fear and didn't need any rest. He was absorbed in the strike day and night.

Once, the chair of the Picketing Committee, who coordinated to keep watch over the shops and prevent any scabs from replacing strikers at work, entrusted him with an important mission. The committee had received a report that there was a home shop set up in a private house far outside of the fur district, and strikebreakers were working there. Avreml was sent to find out who the scabs were and to bring them to the Strike Committee.

Avreml watched the house for a few nights with a group, or *de-le-gei-shen*, of strikers, but the neighborhood was quiet and thinly populated.

---

1   Ben Gold was elected manager of the New York Joint Board in 1925.

2   *The Jewish Daily Forward.*

The delegation had provoked suspicion. No one left or entered the house, and it was clear that whoever was inside the house had noticed them. Avreml withdrew their surveillance for the night, on the understanding that one person from the delegation would return to the house at another time so as not to raise suspicion. As a lone striker, it would be easier to hide from the scabs, who were always on the lookout for strangers.

Avreml took the assignment himself. It was pouring rain that night. The street was dark and desolate, with no one walking about. The windows of both rows of private homes were unlit.

Avreml walked quietly onto the porch of the house. He slowly opened a window and entered. From the front room, he tiptoed through the small corridor, where an electric light glowed faintly. The stairs were on the right of the hallway, nestled against the wall. The back stairwell led down to the cellar, where there were lights on. Holding his breath, he silently walked down the stairs. On the bottom step, he stood completely still, as if paralyzed. There was an entire shop in the cellar. Sewing machines stood in the middle of the room and various kinds of furs lay strewn about the cement floor, but there were no operators there. A long table stood by the wall. A cutter was at the table, and he was cutting. The small windows, facing onto the backyard, were covered in dark heavy fabric.

The cutter working at the table was Avreml's old friend from the early days, the "Socialist" Morris. Worn out and sleepy, he was immersed in his work and hadn't heard that someone had entered the cellar. Avreml coughed. Morris jerked. The knife fell out of his hand. He turned around quickly toward the cough. Avreml was already standing right next to him. Morris was pale with fright.

"Avreml? You?" He was barely able to get the words out. "What are you doing here?"

In a calm, dry tone, Avreml answered, "The union sent me here. I demand you come with me to the union office."

Morris fell apart. He sat down on a chair, sank his face in his hands, and cried openly. When he had calmed down a bit, he told Avreml his story of bankruptcy. His creditors had gotten him arrested on charges of embezzling merchandise from them. It had been a great struggle to manage to save himself from jail. He had *set-tild*, meaning he had worked out a deal in court with his creditors, and now he had to set aside weekly payments according to the judge's order. If he didn't pay up, he would get sent to prison.

"I've gotten myself tangled up in a net, and I can't get myself loose," he said with tears in his eyes. "Those creditors have me caught in a trap. They've got me under their thumb, and they have no mercy. It's only on account of those exploiting fleecers that I've got to scab. Every dollar I earn, I give right over to the creditors. My wife is sick. She's broken down from all these troubles. She's gone out to my brother's farm."

With trembling hands, Morris showed Avreml the receipts from his weekly payments to his creditors. He also showed him invoices from doctors' treatments for his ill wife and letters that his wife had sent him from the farm.

"Avreml," he begged, "stand by me in my hard times. I swear to you on my sick wife, I'll get rid of this scab shop tomorrow and go off to my brother's farm. I promise I'll stay there with my wife until the strike is over."

"Who else is scabbing here?" Avreml asked sternly.

Morris gave him the workers' names, as well as the names of the businesses that were sending work, and the address of the farm where he was going.

"Don't ruin my reputation," he begged. "It's the only thing I have left. Remember Avreml, how I helped you out when you were going through tough times, when you needed a friend's help. I'm the one who brought you into the union. Now I'm asking you a favor. Help me out now when I really need it."

Avreml couldn't even look at Morris. He was overcome with disgust for him. And that feeling of disgust spread over to himself as well, because he could feel how his pity for Morris was overpowering his duty to the union and to the strikers. He couldn't withstand this broken man's begging. Morris, who had been so proud in the old days, was sitting there beaten, a sacrifice to the great business-wolves who devour weak animals in the capitalist jungle.

Against his will, and against his instinct as a trade unionist, Avreml took Morris on his word of honor that he would close up his scab shop and go off to his brother's farm.

Two days later, he telephoned Morris to reassure himself he had kept his word. His heart stopped when Morris picked up the telephone.

"What are you doing at home?" yelled Avreml into the mouthpiece. "Why didn't you leave town?"

Morris answered in an arrogant tone that he wasn't leaving at all. He was staying in New York.

Avreml felt his head spin. He set out for Morris's place burning with anger. When he got near the house, he noticed a policeman there. He could see the whole situation clearly now. That strikebreaker Morris had outmaneuvered him, played him for his sentiments—and he had won. He would rather make an arrangement with creditors than give up strikebreaking. Money was more important to him than his own dignity. Avreml knew he should have understood that and worked it all out, because if he couldn't, well then what kind of union leader was he?

Full of regret and scorn for himself, Avreml went to the union and told the head strike leader the whole story.

5

An important meeting was being held in a room of the Party Building. The members of the regional office and some of the activists of the Furriers Union, Avreml among them, were there. The chair was an experienced party veteran with a great deal of experience in the trade-union movement. He led the gathering calmly, proficiently, and tactfully. He didn't encounter any difficulties, because the others were also calm, earnest, and focused.

"Serious accusations," explained the chair, "have been brought to the party against Comrade Broide. The complainants are Furriers Union activists who are present. The accused Comrade Broide is also present. Comrade N,[1] a union activist, will take the floor. He will bring forth the facts, to build the basis of the accusation."

"As you know comrades," began Comrade N, "the union is engaged in an important and difficult strike. In opposition, we have the bosses, their hired muscle, the police, and the hostile press. *De-tek-tivs* (undercover agents) invade the meeting halls where strikers gather, and they arrest important strike leaders. Corrupt judges, who are working hand in hand with the bosses, send the strikers to *priz-in* and fine them enormous amounts in order to exhaust the strike fund and break the strikers' morale. Our most difficult struggle, however, is turning out to be the one against Socialist obstacles within and without. Their plan is to break the strike, as well as the union, all to discredit the left union leaders. Their newspaper openly agitates for workers to scab. But the strikers have loyalty to the left leadership.

"The party comrades in the union," he continued, "are active day and night on the picket lines and in the various strike committees together with the strikers. With their work, they inspire self-respect and raise the prestige of the party among the strikers. Avreml—I mean Comrade Broide—is one of the most active comrades. You know his merits, and I don't need to belabor them.

---

1 Possibly a reference to Charles Nemeroff of the Furriers Union, who served as the assistant secretary of the Needle Trades Workers Industrial Union, the Communist-affiliated network organized in 1928, where Gold was the secretary.

"A few days ago, Comrade Broide came to me, as the chair of the General Strike Committee, and confided that he had perpetrated a damaging act. I had sent him to investigate a shop. He found a scab there, but instead of bringing him to the union, he let him go. If the strikers found out about this, they would lose their faith in us, and the strike would be greatly weakened. Therefore, I brought this charge against Comrade Broide." Comrade N concluded and sat down.

The chair gave the floor to other union activists. All of them upheld the accusation and supported the complaint against Comrade Broide.

"Comrade Broide," the chair addressed Avreml, "do you comprehend the seriousness of the accusation against you?"

"Yes."

"Do you want to make an explanation? I assure you that the bureau will give you every opportunity to explain the situation."

Looking pale, Avreml got up from his seat. He noticed how everyone's eyes were pointed at him. He moistened his dry lips with his tongue. At first, he lowered his eyes, as if he were looking for something on the floor. But then he straightened himself up and began to speak. He didn't speak about himself as a lawyer would, but as a plaintiff.

"Everything that Comrade N said is correct," he began. "I do comprehend the seriousness of the act I committed. That is why I went to Comrade N and told him the whole truth. I am prepared to accept the appropriate punishment, but I don't want the strike to be damaged by this. The strike . . ."—Avreml's voice choked up—"The strike is the most important thing. I am not important. I don't want to defend myself or justify myself. I would only like for you to know everything about my act, including the personal aspects and the subjective motivations, that moved me to behave in this manner. To that end, please permit me to recount what happened in more detail."

He told of his encounter with Morris on that night, and also about the role Morris had played earlier in his life. His speech was long, and it might have seemed that many of the things which he presented had nothing to do with the matter at hand. But the chair did not interrupt him and the others listened to his speech with deep attention.

"And that, comrades, is the pure truth," ended Avreml. "It is clear that I don't have enough experience, that I am still gullible. This is my error, a grave error, of course. And you should sentence me strictly. I am certain however, that as you do, you will take into account my record as a union activist and a party activist. I have always monitored myself to maintain a spotless party reputation. It is my fault that I allowed myself to be deceived by Morris. I admit that. But comrades, this is not an act of intentional betrayal. I would sooner sacrifice my life than betray the party. I'm done. You can be sure that whatever you decide, I will honor it in a spirit of loyalty to the party and to the labor movement."

The deliberations began. The bureau members discussed the matter calmly, objectively, politically. His comrades didn't see Avreml's error only as a personal act, but also as a symptom of the instability that derives from insufficient Marxist–Leninist knowledge. The case of Comrade Broide, they concluded, should serve as a warning that the party must become more rigorous in the political education of its members.

At the discussion's conclusion, several motions were proposed, and the bureau unanimously decided:

That the party recognizes the loyal and valuable work of Comrade Broide.

That namely because comrade Broide is such an important party activist, he must be made an example for others, not to enter into any compromises with a scab without the knowledge of the union leadership. Therefore, Comrade Broide deserves the sharpest censure, and he is strongly warned against opportunistic deviants.

That if Comrade Broide, or any other comrade, should, in the future, need to make any of his own decisions about his assigned responsibilities, he must bring the matter to the accountable committee, unless it is absolutely impossible.

That Comrade Broide must register for courses in the workers' school[2]

---

2   Possibly a reference to The Jewish Workers University, an adult education program run by the Jewish Section of the Communist Party. It offered classes in politics, economics, Yiddish literature, etc. See Melech Epstein, *The Jew and Communism* (New York: Trade Union Sponsoring Committee, 1959), 209–210. Thanks to Dylan Kaufman-Obstler for the reference.

where he must take English, political economics, trade-unionism, and other important subjects.

That the party bureau sentences him as a Communist and as a party member. Therefore, the handling of Comrade Broide should be brought forth in a deliberation to the entire picketing committee, and the party comrades should use this incident as a lesson for others, to teach strikers about the proper methods of strike leadership.

The chair read out the decisions and made a summary of the entire affair.

"Comrade Broide," he addressed Avreml, "you have a very robust sense of loyalty. That is good. But when a comrade forgets his primary responsibility to his union and his party, even for one moment, due to his loyalty to a personal friend, it could eventually lead to a system of personal favors charged to the labor movement's account. As a Communist you can have only one kind of loyalty—faithfulness to the labor movement, and that means, not least—to the party, because the interests of the labor movement are also the interests of the party. They are one and the same. You, Comrade Broide, put your loyalty to your former friend above your loyalty to your union and your party. I hope you understand your mistake, and I warn you, in a comradely spirit, about that sort of personal loyalty."

Years later, Avreml would be put to an even harder test between personal and party loyalty. At this moment though, he felt strengthened by the party verdict. He was excited, if surprised, by the ruling that he had to enroll in the workers' school and take up serious learning.

6

Avreml met Miriem in the workers' school. She taught his English class. When he first saw Miriem, so charming and petite, he fell in love with her. When she called him to her little desk and wrote his name and address in a book, she reached out her hand and said simply and comradely, "I hope you will be among my best students."

He took her small delicate hand, with its long thin fingers, in his, and a soft shiver ran through his being. She noticed his disorientation and smiled. From that smile, round little dimples emerged in both her cheeks. Two rows of even, white teeth gleamed from her parted mouth. Her intelligent black eyes shot sparks. He answered her smile with a smile, and it rattled him even more.

Miriem was also taken with Avreml as soon as he entered the class. When their eyes would meet, she blushed and felt a strange nervousness. The more she tried to avoid his gaze, the more their eyes joined up. For the first time in her young life, Miriem couldn't subdue her feelings. It was as if she were intoxicated from Avreml's face, which expressed both goodness and masculine strength. She felt a physical need to look at him, to examine his high brow and his head with its curly blond hair.

She thought about Avreml day and night, and every day became more agitated. In class, she forced herself to maintain her typical calm, but she knew that she was only posing, that she was head over heels in love with her handsome student. With her other boyfriends she felt oddly cold and indifferent, not at all like she had earlier, and not at all like her nature. On the nights when she had to teach the class in which Avreml was a student, she worried more than usual about her clothing and how she looked. Sometimes he would be a few minutes late. At those times, Miriem got very nervous, but her mood immediately changed when he arrived. She became lively, cheerful, and talkative. When she began to think he smiled too often and was too friendly with one of the female students in class, she resented it sorely.

Avreml did not at all suspect that Miriem thought about him. He only knew that a new topic had been introduced into his life. From the first time he'd met her, his days and nights had become radiant and light filled. He constantly saw Miriem's beautiful face, her graceful movements, her enchanting smile. His ears didn't stop hearing her voice. He enjoyed thinking about her, and the hour he spent in her class felt like a great holiday for him. If he reminded himself for a moment about his first love and compared Miriem to Rivele, he rejoiced at having been rescued by coming to America.

He didn't even dare to think about whether or not Miriem could love him. But that didn't stop him from giving into his feelings for her. His work in the party and the union became even more gratifying since meeting Miriem. He was a keen learner. He studied in all his free time, not only because he was thirsty for knowledge and to uphold the party's verdict, but also to make a good impression on Miriem. He would meet her at demonstrations and at important party meetings, which made the gatherings even more important. He was no ladies man, and outwardly he behaved with Miriem almost coldly and aloof.

Miriem couldn't stand his self-restraint. She didn't understand why he was so different from all the other men she knew. They showed their pleasure at every meeting and chased after her for dates. A few of them had even declared their love for her. He was the only one who acted so civilly, almost indifferently to her. Of all of them, only Avreml had never made even the slightest attempt to take her out on dates. It hurt her so much that she decided to swallow her pride and arrange an encounter with him, to find out once and for all where things stood between them.

One evening, when class had ended, she casually kept Avreml back and asked him how his studies were going. He didn't suspect anything and answered that his studies were going very well and that she was a very good teacher who helped him a lot. As he was speaking, Miriem slipped into her coat, put on her hat, and said with the same affected coolness, "Comrade Broide, are you leaving, or do you have another class?"

Avreml answered quickly that he was going home. They went out to the street together. On their way, Miriem suggested, with the same cool politeness, that they go to a diner for a coffee. She noticed his delight as he accepted her suggestion and smiled with a barely suppressed triumph.

They settled into a free table and ordered coffee and cookies. Miriem directed the conversation very cautiously. Avreml gladly answered her questions about his union activity, about the great progress the union was making in increasing the comrades' leadership, about the confidence the workers had in the leadership of the union activists, and about the fierce clashes with the troublemakers from the right. She marveled at his talent for explaining complicated union problems in a simple way. He got her truly interested in his efforts, and she didn't notice the clock and how time was flying. When they left the restaurant, it was already late at night. At their parting, she said she had a very nice time over those couple of hours, and that she hoped that he would continue those conversations with her because it was very important for her to become acquainted with these sorts of union problems.

From then on, they met quite frequently. They would take walks together and talk for hours at a time about various topics: about the questions of the labor movement, about the party, about their activities, and about several party leaders. Miriem was certain that sooner or later, Avreml would declare his love to her. She was absolutely sure now that he was in love with her. She understood that his self-restraint came from his shyness and his scant experience with women. It gave her a thrill, and she waited patiently. A few times, she carefully let him understand that she wanted to continue their friendship. But Avreml didn't dare to think that she was in love with him. Miriem often ran out of patience. She wanted to scream, "You foolish boy! You can see I love you even more than you love me, so when are you going to stop being so damn polite?" But she played along in the politeness game. She waited. She was sure the moment would come. He was sure that she liked meeting with him and spending long hours together. But he was scared it was still too early. He worried that Miriem would turn down his proposal and it would end their friendship. So, he decided to delay his declaration of love until he was absolutely certain that he wasn't just deluding himself and that Miriem really did love him.

7

In the party, a fierce conflict surfaced between two factions. Party members divided into opposing camps and neared hostility. Only a small number of members remained more or less neutral, not joining one faction or the other. Party assemblies were the battlegrounds. Party meetings, whether major or minor, stretched until late at night. Each faction accused the other of anti-party activities, of opportunistic deviations, of not voting in accordance with the party's interests but rather in the interests of their own caucus resolutions. Long speeches filled every meeting. Bitter allegations were made on both sides. Each faction had its own program for the party and its work in the mass organizations. Each faction fought vehemently for its programs and made every effort to show how the other faction's programs posed the utmost threat to the party and to the labor movement. The faction leaders stubbornly campaigned for their interpretations of Marxist–Leninist theories and tactics. It grew so extreme that the party became much more occupied by these internal struggles than with its mission to increase the influence of the entire party in the labor movement.

Miriem was one of the leaders of the L[1] faction. Naturally, her conversations with Avreml became discussions of the party's internal issues. Miriem couldn't comprehend why in the world Avreml was one of the neutral comrades. It pained her that she couldn't bring him into the L faction. She became achingly resentful that he had so much loyalty and respect for Comrade F[2] and the other comrades in leadership of the F faction. With his characteristic integrity, Avreml admitted that he still wasn't able to evaluate the theoretical distinctions between the two

---

1   The "right opposition," led by Jay Lovestone, who was removed from leadership of the US Communist Party by Stalin in 1929. By the time of this novel's publication he was an active anti-Communist.

2   William Z. Foster, founder of the TUEL, whom Stalin appointed in place of Lovestone as head of the US Communist party in 1929.

factions, and that only one thing was clear to him: the conflict injured the party, and F and his group were important, competent, faithful party leaders.

The more fiercely the factional struggles blazed in the party, the more embittered Miriem became against the F faction. She would talk to Avreml for hours about the danger that the F faction posed to the party. Avreml didn't agree with her. Miriem would get hysterical. Their conversations mutated into political battles. A few times they promised to avoid party discussions on their dates, but it was impossible to sustain. One time, Miriem reproached Avreml, saying that with his neutrality, he was in fact supporting the F faction, and she implored him that it would be better if he became involved with the L faction. Avreml was torn. He warned her firmly that he wouldn't allow anyone to dictate his affiliations. Hurt, Miriem quickly said goodbye to him and left the restaurant.

Weeks and months passed without Avreml and Miriem meeting again. He missed her terribly. Only now could he feel how strongly he loved her. He just couldn't forgive her position. He continually thought about the lecture the chair had given him in the office about personal loyalty. He remained firmly determined that his love and devotion to Miriem would not block the way of his devotion to the party. He decided that even if he had to give up Miriem entirely, he would remain faithful to his affiliations and to his position in terms of the party situation.

Miriem couldn't stand it. She knew she had behaved inappropriately and marveled at Avreml's restraint. But her factional arrogance and her pride prevented her from making a gesture to reconcile with him. Her longing consumed and tormented her. She went out with her other fellows a few times, but she had lost interest in them. Her party work, the assemblies which kept her up until late at night, the extended factional struggles, and her gnawing longing for Avreml started to undermine her health. She lost weight. Her face turned wan. She became agitated and nervous.

When summer came, her parents pressured her to travel on a long European vacation. Her father, a rich building contractor, pleaded with her to have pity on herself and her mother, and to take a trip to rescue her health. Miriem did not go. She didn't even want to think about going far away from Avreml. Her parents didn't know what was eating up their only daughter. She did, however, agree to go with them to their summer home, which wasn't far from the city, to spend the summer with them.

One day, when Avreml got home, he found a letter on his desk. He took a glance at the envelope. The handwriting was familiar. He ripped open the envelope. Miriem had invited him to visit her and her parents at their summer home. She described its beautiful location by the river and promised that he would have a chance to rest up for a few days because she promised not to speak about party business for anything. Avreml felt revitalized. He reread the letter several times. He was now certain the time had come for him to tell Miriem he loved her dearly. He was sure Miriem wouldn't rebuff him. The next day, he packed his summer things and left to see Miriem.

He was thrown off by the large, luxe house in which Miriem and her parents lived. He had known that Miriem's father wasn't a worker or a poor man, that Miriem had never had to work in a factory, and that her father had supported her through all the best schools. But he hadn't understood that her father was this kind of rich. It disappointed him quite a bit. But with the genial way Miriem's parents related to him and Miriem's warm friendship, he quickly became accustomed to the plush lifestyle and started to feel at home, almost like an old friend of the family.

Miriem was a completely different person at the summer home. She laughed, frolicked, sang, and ran around among the trees and in the deep grass like a child. She spent entire days outside with Avreml until late at night. They swam, played, fished, and walked long stretches. Their skins browned in the warm sun. They became even more friendly and comfortable with each other, and love beamed from their eyes. Miriem's parents could tell they weren't any kind of casual friends. They noticed the drastic transformation that had taken place in their daughter since Avreml's arrival. They came to love this strong, finely built, handsome fellow, and felt glad that their daughter and he had become close.

Finally, Miriem got what she had been waiting for. She and Avreml were sitting on the grass, watching the red sun sinking and reflecting its brilliant colors on the river. All of a sudden, Avreml started speaking. "Miriem, we've spent a few wonderful days together. You'll never know how grateful I am to you for inviting me here. I had thought I would never see you again after that night. I love you very much. If I were your equal, an established professional, and I could support you with a comfortable life, as you are accustomed, I would dare to ask you to marry me."

"You foolish boy," Miriem interrupted him.

A chill coursed through Avreml's body. Miriem was quiet for a minute, and it seemed to Avreml that all was lost. He regretted speaking so openly. He wanted to take back his words, but he was shaken, and didn't know what to say or what to do. Miriem's accusation—*you foolish boy*—rang in his ears like a death sentence. The river lurched. He felt lightheaded. Finally, Miriem broke the silence. She said calmly, "I've waited for this moment for so long. It tore up my heart, waiting so long. I was scared you didn't love me at all."

Avreml felt as though he had woken up from a deep sleep. Impetuously, he turned to face Miriem. Her dark eyes had filled with tears. He grabbed her in his arms, stood up, and lifted her up along with his own body. He nestled her against his broad chest and covered her damp eyes and face with kisses. She heard the hammering of his heart. She held his head in her gentle hands and gave herself over to his lips.

After he tenderly returned her to the grass, she hid her face in her hands, turned toward the grass, and began to cry. Avreml caressed her and, distressed, asked her why she was crying. Sobbing, she explained in broken words that she couldn't control it, this greatest joy of her life.

Returning to the house, they found Miriem's parents sitting on the veranda. Avreml remained standing outside. Miriem ran in quickly and called out for her mother. Mrs. Rubin got up from her seat and remarked to her husband that some kind of news was afoot. When she got in the house, Miriem held her and said, "Mama, I'm going to marry Mr. Broide."

Mrs. Rubin answered right away, "Nu, you should have all the happiness," and called for her husband.

Mr. Rubin received the news with a facial expression showing he couldn't decide if he was pleased or not. He wanted his Miriem to marry a doctor, a lawyer, or a rich businessman. He hadn't expected a match like this. But ultimately, just like his wife, he wished his daughter luck and shouted, "Mr. Broide, what are you standing outside for? Come on in. You're one of us now."

Liquor, wine, and refreshments appeared on the table. Mrs. Rubin didn't take her eyes off Avreml. She settled on the opinion that Miriem had selected well and declared, "You know Mirieml, if I were in your place, I would also choose Broide. He is a fine, handsome young man."

Mr. Rubin, who was drinking, acted hurt and said in jest, "Oh yeah? So you regret marrying me? Now I see how I measure up."

They all laughed heartily.

Mr. Rubin approached Avreml. Teasingly, he warned him about his beautiful capricious daughter, who was used to a life of comfort and having everything prepared for her. Avreml answered, also in a teasing tone, that he was up to the task of getting Miriem accustomed to a worker's lifestyle. Mr. Rubin quipped that Miriem was a fine Communist but didn't know anything about what it means to make a living. Miriem protested.

Mr. Rubin asked, "So, when are you two going to get married?"

Miriem answered, "Tomorrow."

Avreml said he would somehow be able to wait until tomorrow. Mr. Rubin turned toward the practical side of the engagement. He assured Avreml he was pleased with the match, and that if Avreml wanted to stop being a worker and go into business, he wouldn't have to worry about money because Miriem was his precious jewel and he wouldn't skimp on her.

"Miriem," said Mr. Rubin, "has brought me a lot of luck. From the day she was born, I've been making money. Hopefully it will be the same for you."

Avreml let him know that he wasn't going into business, that he would remain a worker, and that he would make due with his wages. Mr. Rubin was a bit displeased, but he thought to himself that there would still be time to discuss the matter.

"If that's so," he said, "then I will be very happy to give you a house I'll build you, as a wedding present."

Avreml felt embarrassed and declined the gift. Mrs. Rubin interjected to say that the two children would live with them. Her house was big enough for ten people, and she wanted to have the children with her so she wouldn't have to wander around such a large house all alone. That talk got too serious, and Miriem suggested postponing the practical issues until the next day.

8

The party's factional conflict blazed ever more fiercely and threatened to break out into a genuine crisis. L and his faction crystallized a program that set aside certain fundamental principles of Marxism's scientific doctrines in relation to capitalist economics, with its cycles of expansion and crisis.[1]

The L faction denied the possibility of an economic crisis in America. According to their program, their theoreticians asserted that no economic crisis would happen in America because the impoverished, industrially underdeveloped southern states continually provided a newly discovered America and unlimited possibilities for building enterprises across the entire country and maintaining high wage standards for workers. To that false and corrupt theory specifically, the party objected.

It got to the point where L and his supporters had to leave the party. The F faction took over party leadership. Several conscientious party activists, who had previously stood with the L faction, openly distanced themselves from the opposition and stayed in the party. The overwhelming majority of members stayed. Only a small group remained with the opposition. Miriem left the party with the L faction.

It was important to establish unity, cohesion, and accountability in the party ranks. It was also necessary to eliminate every influence of the harmful L opposition. The faction's leader organized his followers and began staging open attacks against the party and the Third International.[2] A few of his adherents stayed behind in the party to organize a new caucus and undermine the party from within.

Therefore, it was necessary that each former L faction adherent who stayed in the party openly declare their position. They were called to appear before special committees set up in each neighborhood, and after

---

1 "American exceptionalism." See Le Blanc & Davenport collection, and Zumoff, which explain the 1929 split as more personal and political than theoretical.

2 The direction set by the Soviet-controlled international communist party between 1928 and 1933, which forbade any cooperation with actors outside the approved party line.

brief political discussions, they were instructed to make written declarations of their beliefs and positions. Anyone who refused to make a written statement was expelled from the party.

Avreml was one of the people called to appear before a special party committee. He declared he was sticking with the party, even though his wife had left with the L faction. He made it clear how difficult it was for him to tolerate his wife's anti-party tendencies, but that she had absolutely no influence on his own convictions and loyalty to the party. He declined to make a written declaration denouncing the L adherents as traitors. That, he explained, would certainly lead to a break with his wife.

Avreml was expelled from the party. Miriem was happy about it. She goaded her husband with talk about how the party was ruled by a bureaucracy that wanted to control its members' private lives. Avreml didn't argue with her. He sided with the party and understood that the party had the right to be suspicious of a member who lived with a woman who was active in the anti-party opposition. He didn't want to argue with Miriem because he was sure that no good would come from any quarrel. To him it was clear that party members' personal lives couldn't be separated from their party lives. He understood that the party had a right, and even an obligation, to influence members whose personal relationships could damage the party's reputation. He knew from his own experience that in the mass organizations, the workers have to think of Communists' personal lives as a reflection of Communist morale and accountability, and that the party's enemies are always looking to take advantage of the smallest blot in a Communist's personal life in order to smear the entire party. But he didn't talk to Miriem about that. He wanted to stay clear of fights. From experience, he knew they couldn't discuss their sharp differences of political opinions in a calm way and without personal bitterness. He wanted to avoid political conflicts with Miriem, whom he loved very much. Even though he knew the party had been obligated to expel him, he started to resent how his party comrades refused to honor his own loyalty to the party and pressured him so brutally to denounce his own wife.

Miriem knew Avreml was upset and hurt. The way he had completely given up on talking to her about the political situation and stewed silently started to worry her. She looked for a way to calm him. She shared the secret with him that L was seriously considering a return to the party with his group. Avreml felt revitalized. He believed her because he wanted to believe it and because it would offer a clear way out of his own mixed-up situation. After all, he thought, L had been a party leader for so many years. He must be loyal to the progressive labor movement, and the party would be glad to prevent an open battle. The more he thought about it the more he became convinced it was possible to eliminate the strife and build unity. It would be good for the party indeed!

An oddly strained relationship of careful love had developed between Avreml and Miriem. Miriem worried that sooner or later, Avreml would blame her for his getting thrown out of the party and cut off from his friends and comrades. She feared he wouldn't be able to endure it and would erupt in a rage destroying her entire life. So she became ever more gentle with him, as if she were trying to ease his pain with her gentleness.

And Avreml, for his part, didn't want Miriem to be upset that she was the reason he had been expelled. That's why he hoped that maybe on his account, she would refrain from open tirades and attacks against the party. He understood that she was trying to compensate for his major loss with her exaggerated gentleness. He felt sorry for her, and also enjoyed how kindly she was treating him through his tough times, so he reciprocated her gentleness. They both knew that the way they were treating each other was contrived and calculated, but they didn't even try returning to authenticity.

One time, in a very careful way, Miriem asked Avreml to go with her to an important meeting of the L group. She told him the rumor that L was going to make a report on his attempts to bring the group back to the party. Avreml didn't want to go, but she implored him and begged him to do it for her. Due to the excessive gentleness that was now managing their relationship, he couldn't refuse her. And moreover, he was curious to find out more about the possibilities of getting back into the party.

At the meeting, Avreml sat off in a corner. He felt a strange alienation among the defunct comrades. He answered his acquaintances' greetings with a curt, silent nod of his head. When their greetings became too open, he buried his eyes in a newspaper until the meeting started.

The meeting chair was G,[3] a former party leader. He began his speech with a short announcement about the success of the L group and said the group was growing in size and influence, that the party was shrinking, and that soon there wouldn't be anyone left to expel. And then he launched into a ferocious attack against the party leadership, the Third International, and the leaders of the Soviet Union.

Avreml felt like he was sitting on hot coals. He couldn't believe his own ears. He had only heard this kind of talk from the party's wildest enemies. He had heard these kinds of revolting accusations and vulgar remarks against the Communist Party from White Guard enemies. He absolutely could not comprehend that G was capable of such open and unashamed treason. He felt chewed up. It took all his strength not to scream out, "Traitor! That's how a provocateur talks!"

He tried to calm himself. Of all these people, G was a man who had never really been a leader. It hadn't been a secret in the party that he didn't know much theory and had even less political smarts. He had never been any kind of mass leader. If it hadn't been for this unfortunate factional struggle, he wouldn't have gotten a chance to play this important leadership role. He had practically been foisted on the party by his caucus. That's why Avreml decided to ignore this particular political ignoramus's speech. Even his group's sycophants called G "the L Caucus's Drummer" because of his booming voice.

Avreml did a lot of waiting for L's great announcement on the business of returning to the party. But he remained bitterly disappointed. L made the same kind of provocateur speech as his sidekick G, but in a sly way, wrapped up in "theory" and verses from Marx and Lenin, which he tangled and translated to serve him.

He conveyed his ostensible regret that the party was dying, that the Third International was endangering the great revolution in the Soviet Union. He talked for a long time. Avreml smiled. He was proud that he wasn't getting fooled by this emissary of political falsehoods and acrobatic

---

3   Benjamin Gitlow, staff labor organizer for the Communist Party of the USA, briefly editor of the *Morning Freiheit*. Became a leader of the Lovestone faction, and then a vocal anti-Communist.

The Drummer from the L Caucus spoke like a provocateur.

arguments. Avreml could understand now why the party was so determined to clean out all the L followers. He had now heard from L's own
mouth the kind of talk that provocateurs used to destroy the party. *Wow*,
thought Avreml, *how is it possible that these people were party leaders so
recently?* He started to understand that with leaders like that, the party
had actually been in serious danger.

When L finished, Avreml couldn't take any more and wanted to leave
the hall. But he heard his Miriem getting called to the platform, so he
stayed in his seat. A thought flashed through his mind—*Miriem will let
them have it! She'll make a mess of them!*—but to his astonishment and
deep anguish, Miriem spoke in the same spirit and in the same tone as
the preceding speakers. Avreml bit his lip. Miriem's words cut him like
knives. "Miriem, Miriem," his lips whispered quietly. He felt like he was
sinking. The people in the hall danced up and down in his eyes. He looked
for something to hold onto so he wouldn't fall off his chair. Suddenly, he
heard his Miriem's sharp voice carrying through the hall, "A true Communist must stay loyal to their ideals and principles, even when they must
pay the highest price for them."

Avreml awoke, as if from sleep. "You're right Miriem," he said softly.
He immediately slipped out of the hall. Now he knew what to do. He
headed home, driven by a terrible hurtling force.

9

Avreml arrived home, sat down at his desk, and wrote:

Dear Miriem:

This evening, in your speech at your meeting, you said that a true Communist must stay loyal to their ideals and principles, even when they must pay the highest price for them. I agree with you.

Therefore you'll understand why I'm leaving you. If I continued on with this life, I would be acting like a coward and a hypocrite. I would end up hating myself, and I would stop loving you.

It's going to be very hard for me to live without you, but I can't live under one roof with you, a party enemy. If you decide to leave the traitors, I'll come running back to you. If not, you'll have to forget about me.

Thank you Miriem, for the beautiful sunny days, and the great joy you brought to my life from the first day I met you. It's a shame our great joy has been ruined. But there is no other way.

Avreml.

He put the letter on the table and left the house right away. He wandered aimlessly around unfamiliar streets for a long while. He didn't think about anything. He couldn't think. His thoughts were all mixed up, making no sense, like in a dream. He couldn't follow any of them to a conclusion. Bits and fragments of the speeches he had heard at the meeting rang in his ears. He heard his Miriem's words afresh: "a Communist must stay loyal to their ideals. . . ." He kept on mumbling the last words he had written to Miriem: "There is no other way."

A terrible exhaustion hit him. His body became heavy, like it was full of lead. He could barely move his feet. It was already late at night. He looked around and noticed he was in a neighborhood far from his home.

He went into a little restaurant. It wasn't very bright or very clean. He ordered some food and coffee. The waiter murmured secretively that if he wanted a drink, he could get one. Avreml nodded his head. When he had finished his first shot, he grimaced from the strong, bitter taste. Then he ordered a second. The liquor refreshed him. He ordered another. The waiter told him he had to pay for liquor after each drink. Avreml smiled, gave the waiter a fin, and asked for a whole bottle. He poured one glass after another right into himself. When it became difficult for him to sit on the chair, the waiter led him out of the restaurant, leaned him against a nearby wall, and left him there.

Avreml wobbled. He didn't know what was happening to him. He tried with all his might to stay on his feet. Everything was spinning around him in weird circles and he rocked with the buildings and the entire street. The late-night passersby glanced with a smile at the drunk who was climbing up the walls.

A streetwalker approached him. She noticed his delicate face in the lamplight and said, more to herself than to him, "Poor guy, you've sauced yourself up with poison. You'll be lucky if you don't drop dead."

She took him by the arm and held him up so he wouldn't fall. He turned his head to her, wanting to say something, but his lips were paralyzed. He wanted to give her a smile, but he couldn't.

"Come with me, you big dummy," she said in a commanding voice. She put her arm around him and directed him. With wobbling steps, he dragged himself to follow her. She brought him to a dark side street and worked hard to get him into her room, pushing and dragging. She laid him out on her wide bed next to the wall. He groaned, mumbled something, and lifted his hands, though they fell back down on the bed like pieces of wood. In no time, he fell asleep like a stone. She took off his shoes and, with some effort, his jacket, untied his necktie, spread open his collar, and covered him with a blanket. When she had finished her work, which she did with skillful, experienced hands, she knocked softly on the door adjoining her room.

"Jack," she called quietly. "It's me, Florence. Come in here."

The door opened. A tall hardy guy with a big head, thick lips, and a

"Come with me, you big dummy," she said and put her arm around him.

flat nose, slid silently into the room. He wasn't wearing a jacket, and his sleeves were rolled up.

"So you brought home another dead guy," Jack said to Florence in a hoarse voice, taking a look at Avreml, who was sleeping like a corpse. "Where do you find them?"

"Aw, you're the one who gets chiseled by them, you sorry thing," answered Florence. Jack's black eyes flashed at her, and he said hostilely, "You shut your mouth!"

He ripped the blanket off Avreml, lifted him up with one hand, and with the other, patted his pockets. He pulled out a leather wallet from one of them. He opened the wallet and found what he was looking for: money, tens and twenties. Satisfied, he rumbled, "Not bad."

Florence turned around and took a look in the wallet. Jack yelled at her, "What are you sticking your nose in for?" He put the wallet in his back pocket and ordered, "Get rid of him as soon as he comes back to life. But don't momma him. He could think this is an orphanage and you're going to adopt him. Send him out to the fresh air, and soon. Got it? If he starts crowing, give a knock on the door."

He left the room.

When Avreml woke up, it was already midday. He sat up in the bed, held his head in both hands, and called out sleepily, "Miriem!"

"Good morning," answered Florence, who was lying in the bed.

Avreml hastily turned his head toward the direction from which the "good morning" came. When he saw Florence, he immediately jumped out of the bed. He quickly buttoned up his shirt, grabbed his jacket, which was hanging on the back of a chair, and started looking for his hat.

"You don't have a hat," said Florence. "You probably lost it wherever you were drinking."

"Huh?" asked Avreml. Mechanically, he checked his pockets. His wallet was missing. Florence moved under the covers. Avreml stood in the middle of the room, put his hands in his pants pockets, and said, "Listen to me, there was money in my wallet. You can have it. But there were also some pieces of paper in my wallet. Give them to me. You don't need them."

Florence got out of bed, tied her kimono belt tightly, covering her plump body, and knocked on the door. In the next second, Jack was in the room.

"Huh?" growled Jack in his hoarse voice. "What's going on here?"

Florence told him that the guest had cooked up a frame job on her and was saying she had taken his wallet.

"That's how he thanks me for picking him up dead drunk from the gutter, bringing him home, and giving him my own bed," she said.

Avreml turned to Jack, "Mister, I don't want the money from my wallet. She can have the money for herself. I'm just asking for her to give back the few pieces of paper in there. She doesn't need them. They're worthless to her. If she just gives those back to me, I'll go home."

"And if not, what are you going to do?" asked Jack. "Get out of here, if you want to stay alive in this world."

Avreml caught onto the racket. He had heard, and also read, about the methods of the underworld. He sat down on a chair and calmly told Jack, "Buddy, you can't scare me. I'm not leaving until I get my things back."

"Huh?" growled Jack cruelly. "You want me to call the cops?"

"Call them," answered Avreml.

"Oh yeah? So you're a tough guy are you?" He grabbed Avreml by the arms and pushed him to the door.

Avreml shoved him off and sat back down on the chair. Jack turned white in anger. His black eyes blazed. He hit Avreml in the face. Avreml fell over with the chair.

"So, are you leaving now, or do you want more?"

Avreml got up with effort, went toward the door with small, measured steps, keeping watch of Jack, who was standing like a scratched animal. Suddenly, he stopped, and with extraordinary deftness, punched Jack in his hardy mug. He fell back onto the bed behind him. He started getting up from the bed, but Avreml met him with a second wallop to the face. It echoed through the room. Jack fell back onto the bed. Avreml held him up with his left hand and hammered Jack's head with his right.

Florence ran to Avreml and yelled, "Let him go. Here, take your wallet."

She quickly drew out the wallet from Jack's pocket and gave it to

Avreml. Jack lay knocked out on the bed. His face was swollen, blood oozing from his mouth.

Avreml opened the wallet. It was all in order. He put the wallet in his pocket and went to the door.

"You're a fine guy," said Florence angrily. "You're not even going to pay me for the lodging."

Avreml took out a ten-dollar note from his wallet and threw it on the table. He thought for a moment, put another ten-spot on the table, and left the building.

The fresh air revived him. He got into a taxi and told the driver where to take him. He got out on a familiar street and went into a restaurant where he ordered food and black coffee. Heartsick, he sat at the little table. He remembered what had happened to him. He reminded himself about the letter he had left on the desk at home, about wandering the streets, about the dirty little restaurant where he had gotten drunk. But for the life of him he couldn't remember how he had fallen into that room. He thought, *Damn, what have I done over the past few hours?*

Now he regretted getting into the fight with that hoodlum. What would he have done if he had had a knife or a revolver even? Things like that happen. He could have gotten arrested if one of the neighbors had called the police. "What was I thinking?" he asked himself. The whole story could have been written up in the papers. That would be some fine news story! Why didn't he think about that earlier? He was lucky he had gotten out of it smoothly. But what would have happened if he had gotten mixed up in an ugly scandal? What had he done all that for?

Abruptly, Avreml shuddered. *My party book! My party book!* He cringed, took out his wallet, and looked inside. His party book was there. He breathed freely. *But I'm not even a member of the party*, he thought. *Why did I fight like that for the book?*

He pushed aside the emptied coffee cup and answered for himself. "I fought for my party book because the party is important to me, because it's my party. That's why I left Miriem. I've got to get back in the party. To be active again. Back to my comrades. The sooner the better. Today even. Yes, tonight. No, now! Don't put it off. I will write a declaration right there in the party office. Those people are traitors, a danger to the labor movement. We've got to combat them with no pity."

He left the restaurant and strode with firm steps to the party office. He drew in the fresh air deeply. He felt immediately better. His errors would be corrected very soon. He would be Comrade Broide once again, the loyal, active party member. Yes, that's how it had to be. There was no other way.

10

Another strike broke out in the fur-goods industry. The streets where the fur workshops and stores were concentrated became weapons stockpiles. Policemen filled the entire neighborhood. The bluecoats stood by each building, billy clubs in hand. On both sides of each street, mounted police stood watch. Their trained, well-fed horses understood each of their rider's movements. Policemen in small white-painted automobiles rode back and forth around the streets. Undercover agents creeped into corners and examined each person who walked by with seasoned eyes.

Long rows of strikers marched up and down both sides of the streets. Those were the *pi-kets*. A sign hung on the breast and back of each picket with words "WE DEMAND OUR CONSTITUTIONAL RIGHT TO BELONG TO OUR UNION. WE DEMAND UNION WAGES AND UNION CONDITIONS." An intense anxiety took over the entire neighborhood. Any slight murmur or high innocent voice provoked a shudder among the pickets and the police.

The strikers' faces were washed in a determination that the bosses knew well: a determination formed in suffering, in poverty, in a deep objection to unjust wrongs.

Avreml marched slowly with a group of strike leaders. Here and there, he hung back and talked to strikers and committee members, hearing out their brief reports and giving them instructions to strengthen the picket lines where necessary. At one building, which had fur shops on all of its thirty-two floors, Avreml hung back and talked with the *styu-ardz* (union representatives) from the shops and with the strikers.

Suddenly, as if from out of the ground, a large black automobile drove up and parked across from the giant building where Avreml was talking with the pickets. The automobile's doors opened and several tall, brawny men burst onto the street.

"Here he is," one of them pointed at Avreml, who was ringed by the strikers. They eagerly charged at him, slicing a path through the pickets. They chopped at the strikers' heads and bodies with pieces of iron.

"GANG-STERS!" the cry split the air. The streets rumbled. From all directions, hundreds of strikers charged in the direction of the scream. Policemen ran with them. Others banged on the streets' hard asphalt with their clubs. Their banging carried and amplified through the entire neighborhood. It was a signal to other policemen, who threw themselves in a wild stampede to come and help their comrades. With nervous fingers, several policemen took out their steel whistles, which hung on steel chains from their pockets, and whistled with all their might. The small white police cars rushed in from all sides and deafened the air with their squealing sirens. The buildings' windows opened and men and women stuck out their heads to find out what was happening.

It had begun. When the police arrived on the scene where the bloody attack had occurred, the gangsters were already throttled by a circle of a hundred strikers, who stood one against another, as if hammered from one piece of material. Inside the ring, workers' hands, muscled like iron beams with steel fingers, held the gangsters by their hands, feet, and heads so they couldn't budge one bit. The workers ripped away the rods of iron that the gangsters had brought and used them against the gangsters.

The policemen, tall and strong, tried to break through the strikers' firm line with their shoulders, but without success. They held their clubs by the ends with both hands, and with the round bare wooden sections, beat the strikers in the dead centers of their backs. To the workers it felt like their backs were breaking, their bodies splitting in half. They screamed in pain, but the police still couldn't break through the ring. They went wild and started clubbing the strikers on their legs and bodies. Double the screams ripped through the air. Women strikers shrieked hysterically. The mounted police rushed up and ran into the crowd of workers. The riders made commands to the horses; the horses held themselves back, like they wanted to avoid treading on people. But when they felt the jabs in their ribs, they obeyed. With the entirety of their powerful backsides, the horses forced themselves into the ring of people and ripped it up. Many workers fell to the ground, and the horses trampled them with their horseshoes. With a squealing wild roar, a large police wagon launched tear gas bombs. Policemen got out quickly and set themselves in a firm line right by the wagon, ready for battle.

When the police had finally managed to cut through the ring, it was

With their horses, mounted police drove into the crowd of workers.

already too late. Four gangsters lay on the asphalt beaten and bloodied. Three other roughed-up gangsters who could still stand on their feet were escorted away by several policemen. An ambulance arrived. Doctors in white uniforms dealt with the knocked-out gangsters lying on the ground. Then they carried them into the ambulance on cots and drove the gangsters to the hospital.

The wounded strikers were immediately taken to the union office by other strikers. From there, they were driven by automobile to private doctors. Avreml was arrested together with ten other strikers. He had been hit hard. His face was swollen. Blood dripped from his nose and mouth. The arrestees were brought to court. The gangsters, whom the police had taken away from the scene of the fight, were not in the court-room. They had disappeared, as if by magic. The other gangsters were lying in the hospital.

When the trial began, it was clear that the *dis-trikt-at-toyr-ni* (prose-cutor) was determined to send Avreml to prison. He presented witnesses who swore they had seen and heard Avreml inciting others, and that he himself had participated in the fight. A tall, brawny detective with a red face and small eyes swore he had seen Avreml fighting with a piece of iron in his hand. The main witnesses against Avreml were a manufac-turer, who was known as a bitter opponent of the union, and his *for-man* (shop overseer), a Nazi who had once paraded through the shop in a Nazi uniform.

The union brought witnesses who testified that Avreml had been standing with the strikers from the building and conducting a peaceful conversation; that the gangsters, who started the fight, had not been with the skilled workers; that they had driven up in an automobile and attacked the workers with pieces of iron. The union's lawyer revealed to the court that the boss had been waging a twenty-year fight against the union and that the foreman was a Nazi, a Hitler agent who had openly declared his wish that Hitler would conquer America and eradicate the unions and the Jews.

The union lost. The boss, the Nazi, and the district attorney won. Avreml was found guilty.

Before the judge gave the verdict, the district attorney read a long list of illegal acts, which Avreml had allegedly committed over several years, to the court. He read it in a loud voice and with a dramatic effect.

"First of all, Broide has been arrested many times, always in connection with strikes and other kinds of labor unrest. Second, he had been arrested at several labor demonstrations, which were inspired by the Communist Party.

"Third, he had been arrested in connection with one of the hunger marches, when the jobless, answering the call from the Communist Party, marched on Washington to demand the establishment of government unemployment insurance.[1]

"Fourth, he had been arrested for leading a demonstration of the jobless to city hall and demanding more municipal relief.

"Fifth, he had been arrested when he and others, in an illegal procedure, returned furniture to a neighbor, who had not paid rent due to unemployment, and had been evicted by the owner through a legal process.

"Sixth, he had been arrested when he led mass demonstrations at the Italian and German consulates, where the demonstrators wore signs with insulting inscriptions against the governments of Germany and Italy, and he, Broide, gave a speech from the steps of the German consulate, disobeying police orders, demanding that our country break off relations with Germany. Thereby, he almost drew our government into a major disgrace.

"As you see, *Yur On-or* (Mr. Judge)," said the district attorney, "Broide is a professional agitator, a troublemaker, and a serious danger to society."

In order to demonstrate Broide's depraved character even more clearly, the district attorney added, "I want to inform you, Your Honor, that he does not live with his wife, and that he rejected his father-in-law's offer—a wealthy, honorable citizen—to set him up in business and invest the necessary capital. As you see, Your Honor, Broide chose the way of lawbreaker as his profession. I insist, therefore, that he receive the maximum punishment according to our statutes."

The judge asked Avreml if he had anything to say before he issued his verdict. Avreml responded that everything the district attorney had

---

1   In Wilmington in 1933, police raided a rally at a church on the way to a hunger march in Washington, DC, and arrested and jailed Ben Gold among others.

recounted about his activities was true; he had participated in many strikes and in demonstrations for the jobless, who were dying from hunger, and whose wives and children were sick and had no money to pay a doctor or buy medicine; that it was criminal how in our great, wealthy country there was no social security for the workers, who get thrown out of workplaces in every economic crisis and suffer hunger and poverty.

"It is also true," said Avreml, "that I led a mass demonstration at the German consulate building. The Nazi government murders Jews and has eradicated the unions, imprisoned the bravest freedom fighters in concentration camps, and is preparing to ignite a firestorm of war over the entire world."

And furthermore, he said, "It is true, I don't live with my wife because she is an active enemy of my party and of the labor movement. And I did turn down my rich father-in-law's offer to set me up in business because I don't want other people to work for me. I am proud of my activities as a member of my union and my party. Arrests and persecutions haven't scared me off before, and they won't scare me off now. My activities are not illegal. The Constitution of our great country guarantees every citizen the right to protest injustice, and I consider it my duty to fight for a better America, one that can guarantee security and freedom to all its sons and daughters."

The judge sentenced Avreml to eighteen months in prison and announced his deep regrets that the law didn't permit him to send a criminal like him away for life.

The workers desperately protested the brutal sentence, but Avreml was sent off to prison. When he had completed his jail time and returned, the workers held a big celebration. The union office was packed in the middle of the day. Everyone shoved in to catch a glimpse of Avreml and welcome him back.

The union hosted a banquet to celebrate the liberation of one of its best and most active members, and it grew into a magnificent street demonstration. The union's leaders, as well as representatives from other labor organizations, greeted Avreml and extolled his courageous behavior.

When Avreml, after an extended ovation, finally began to speak, he said, "Thank you, comrades, for your enthusiastic reception. It is very good to be with you in freedom. Prison is not very comfortable. The difficult, monotonous life there is intended to bury the convict's courage and to weaken his fighting spirit, along with his health. But that kind of punishment has little effect on the loyal son of his class and his people.

"The urge to protest against injustice, and the firm desire to struggle against those who oppress and subjugate the people, do not weaken in prison but grow stronger. A Communist's fortitude and fighting spirit become armor plated and invigorated by his thirst for true freedom and justice for all, and by his deep belief that the victory of the common man is unstoppable. Now that I'm free again I will try to make up for those eighteen lost months by working twice as hard. I know that I owe the movement eighteen months of organizing and I will make good on my debt. A debt like that is a privilege to repay."

11

When the Spanish call for help went out to the entire world to stop the murderous fascists, Avreml joined one of the first groups of volunteers and traveled to Spain to battle the fascist beasts.

From time to time, the union activists received news from Avreml. According to his scant reports, Avreml had distinguished himself in quite a few battles and become beloved by the Spanish and foreign fighters. He was promoted to a high rank. He was slightly wounded a few times but always rushed back to the front lines. He led several missions requiring strength, steady nerves, and a clear head. The experiences he had accumulated in the labor movement proved useful to him on the blood-soaked killing fields of Spain as well. He fought, and he also inspired his comrades in the fight.

Avreml wrote only one letter to his comrades in America. It was his first and last letter. He wrote:

Dear Comrades:

By the time you receive this letter, I will no longer be among the living. Tonight, on instructions from headquarters, I will rendezvous with comrades who have volunteered for a mission to defend one of our most important positions, down to the last man and down to the last drop of blood. You can be sure, comrades, that each member of our group will carry out our orders.

We know that none of us will survive. But we also know that our lives will protect many other lives, protect the freedom not only of the Spanish people but of all people, including our America and the Jewish people. "No pasarán!" is our motto, and as long as we live, we are determined that the fascists will not break through.

The international comrades here are fighting like lions. But we are nothing compared to the Spaniards. They are genuine heroes. They laugh in the face of death. Their hatred for the enemy is as strong as their love for their people and their land.

But a heroic fighting spirit alone is not enough. They need weapons to repel the murderous fascist gangs, who are getting their munitions from Hitler and Mussolini. Give us arms, and we will destroy the Spanish fascists and kill every Italian fascist and every German Nazi who sets foot on Spanish soil.

Give us arms, and we will save the Spanish people and the entire world from the fascist plague. The Spanish comrades can't understand why the democratic peoples remain indifferent to this great crisis for the Spanish people. They say that even a blind man can see this is the beginning of an enormous tragedy that is growing to threaten the entire world. If Hitler and Mussolini win in Spain, it will mean fascism triumphs not only against the Spanish people, but against freedom everywhere!

What should I say to these heroic sons of the Spanish people when they ask me why democratic, freedom-loving America has decided to forbid the Spanish people from buying weapons? Chamberlain's game is clear: He wants to sacrifice Spain so the Nazis will invade the Soviet Union. But why should America play along with that tragic ploy? And why should France commit suicide playing along with the farce of non-intervention? Isn't it clear to the Socialists in France that the death of free Spain is also the demise of free France?

The Spanish are heroes, but they need arms. Only the Soviet Union is helping the unfortunate Spanish people. Only the Soviet Union is sending them ships with food, medical supplies, and weapons. But it takes a long time for Soviet ships to reach Spanish shores. Many of them are sunk by Hitler's and Mussolini's submarines.

Spain must get more help. Help from America, from France, and from England could save Spain and the whole civilized world.

Time won't wait. Soon, our group, in the dark of night, will slip out of the hideout where we've been cleaning our guns and preparing to take our positions. I am sure that whatever comes to pass, you comrades will sense your duty and strive with all your might to save the world from these fascist bandits.

They held their position for as long as it was necessary, for as long as their munitions and breath lasted.

I know my hours are numbered. I'm using my last free minutes to express to all of you my deepest gratitude and love. Give my love to our party, which patiently taught and trained me, and showed me the way.

Be well comrades. Death to the fascist enemy! Down to the last man and the last drop of blood—that's our order, and it will be fulfilled.

In warm solidarity,

Your Comrade, Avreml Broide

Avreml and his group carried out their orders. For as long as Avreml and his unit were able to move a muscle, the fascists couldn't break through. With their machine guns, and a few times with their bayonets, they burned holes in the fascist lines. They held their position for as long as it was necessary, for as long as their munitions and breath lasted—down to the last man, down to the last drop of blood.

Madrid was saved. No one from Avreml's group survived, but Madrid was saved.

Reinforcements arrived just before dawn. The fascists retreated. Comrades found Avreml at his machine gun. He was still alive. Others in his group were still alive. They were taken to a hospital. And the hospital didn't have enough medical supplies.

Even those hardened Spanish fighters, who laughed in death's face, couldn't hold back their grief when they heard that Comrade Broide, the American freedom fighter, had died.

Translator's Acknowledgments

This project began at the Yiddish Book Center, first when I encountered the digitized novel on its website, and then through the excellent support and training of its translation fellowship. The comradeship of my fellow translators, and especially of my wise and gracious mentor Faith Jones, guided me through the art and discipline and relieved my isolation during that first year of quarantine. Many more translators and researchers informed my work. Elissa Sampson at the Kheel Center of Cornell University produced an excellent, perfectly timed symposium on the Yiddish Left and helped me appreciate the treasures of their archives, which include the Furriers Union's and the International Workers Order's papers. Hanna Kipnis King spent hours in the New York Public Library's microfilm department scanning the *Morning Freiheit* for me. Most of all, I acknowledge my gratitude to my parents. To my mother, the multilingual literary critic who celebrated Avreml's worth and assisted at every step, and to my father, the Marxist historian who can't help me so directly anymore but clearly provides the foundation.